Types
of
Everlasting
Rest

To Susan, thank you for a
very relaxing interview!

Clio Gray

TWO RAVENS
PRESS

Published by Two Ravens Press Ltd
Green Willow Croft
Rhiroy
Lochbroom
Ullapool
Ross-shire IV23 2SF

www.tworavenspress.com

ISBN: 978-1-906120-04-7

British Library Cataloguing in Publication Data. A CIP record for this book can be obtained from the British Library.

Designed and typeset in Sabon by Two Ravens Press.
Cover design by David Knowles and Sharon Blackie, based on a photograph by Nikita Tiunov.

Printed on Forest Stewardship Council-accredited paper by Biddles Ltd., King's Lynn, Norfolk.

The publisher gratefully acknowledges subsidy from the Scottish Arts Council toward the publication of this book.

 Scottish
Arts Council

About the Author

Clio Gray was born in Yorkshire, brought up in Devon and has been living in Scotland for the past fifteen years, where she works at her local library. She has won many prizes for her short stories, most notably the Scotsman/Orange Award in 2006. Her first novel, *Guardians of the Key*, a historical mystery, was published by Headline in 2006; the sequel, *The Roaring of the Labyrinth*, will be published in August 2007.

Acknowledgements

Some of the short stories in this collection have been published previously in magazines or anthologies. They are:

I Should Have Listened Harder, winner of the Scotsman/Orange Short Story Prize 2006 and published in the resulting anthology entitled *Work,* is reproduced by permission of Polygon, an imprint of Birlinn Ltd (www.birlinn.co.uk)
Damascene Cure: broadcast on BBC Somerset Radio 21st Feb 2005
Hinkelmann Hits the Cellar: published in The New Writer, Sept/Oct 2005
Nil Sorsky & the Walrus: published in The New Writer, Nov/Dec 2005
The Rake-Maker's Garden: published on www.jbwb.co.uk, Sept. 2004
Of Phlegrean Fields: shortlisted for the Sean O'Faolain Prize 2004, and published in the *Southwords* anthology
Does God Play Dice?: published by BCSA, 2004
BP's Boys: published in BCSA Review, 2006
The Caponsiation of Edgardo de Pucci: published in the **MacAllan/Scotland on Sunday Short Story Collection** vol 4 (Polygon, 2002)

Contents

Nil Sorski & the Walrus

I'm in the pillory at Cholmogory having just had my ears sliced off. We are one month into winter, thank God, so the cold has numbed the pain. Even the English rope-traders, who founded the town and run the courts according to their own rules, are not so cruel as to find you thieving in summer. All trials are put off till the first snows – at least when the ear-chopping sentence is the likely result, as it always is when found guilty of theft. It would be a different story if you got caught by the walrus-hunters who live up on the coast. They'd ask no leave, just string you over some thorn bush in the swamp and leave you to the mosquitoes. Mercy is not something they're familiar with, either at work or with friends, let alone strangers. At least we get to keep our feet on the ground, even if most of the year it's frozen. The hunters though, they take off onto the White Sea and up the Kola coast any time the water's clear. They'll damp up at first fog and never dry out till journey's end, which might be months. They get stuck in ice-floes, flipped by whales and wind, drowned, starved or just plain frozen to death, most of which they could have done without leaving home. Then there's the walrus: fifteen foot of fury hanging from your gaff, your bones vibrating with their bellows, their mouths waiting to snap you like a seal, your fingers shivering on the harpoon hoping you'll hit just right and not make them angrier than they already are. You want to get them well dead before you hack off their tusks and use their intestines to make raincoats. Knee-high in blubber and blood, tearing at the skin, hacking through the muscle. Slicing up the gut is bloody hard work – I know, I've tried it – and slitting the stomach pure stinks. But if you're lucky, it's full of cardium-cockles and then you've made a fortune – they love them on the dining tables of Moscow. No such luck for me. I lasted barely a month before I had to be put ashore at Gremikha, sick as a man can be without dying. I spent the rest of the season boiling tusks up with vinegar and unrolling them – which is still hard work if not bloody, and makes your fingers look like boiled cabbage. But at least you kept your feet on the ground and the food in your belly stayed there. And I learned something else, apart from the reek and rip of it all – they don't have ears, those walrus. Or if they do, they're hidden somewhere on the inside.

Someone is lifting my head, sending a pink icicle shivering into my beard.

'Okay, Sylvester, time to go.'

It's Bernard. He removes the bolt-pins and lifts the beam from my neck and wrists. I'm frozen stiff as the pillory-pole and stay in position: arms in front of me slacked at the elbows; neck craned forward, the top of my back a bell-curve, the pillory having been built for shorter men than me. Bernard throws me over his shoulder, a shape into which I am perfectly bent, and carts me off to our cabin to wrap me in sealskins and fill me with vodka-laced borscht.

'Not too bad, then?' It's Bernard again. I've thawed out a little, but am still bowed in front of the fire, my head bleeding into a straw-stuffed cushion. He's obviously shouting from the exaggerated way he's moving his mouth, and through the scabs and the bandages I can just make out the words. Or maybe I read them. Either way, I try to sit up, but keep losing my balance and have to lie down again. I know that this will pass: like sea-sickness, my legs will learn to adjust and I'll soon be up on my feet. After a slicing, you're allowed a week or two before you're back to the factory, jute-dust everywhere: in your nose and hair and clothes and eyes. We wear goggles, like the Lapps showed us, with crosses instead of slits to protect our eyes, but that dust gets everywhere no matter how hard you try. Still, no doubting the goggles are useful against the glare of the snow, and they're free, courtesy of the management. They're not all bad, those English. Been settled here for hundreds of years and you'd only know they're English because they drink beer before their vodka. That's something we Prussians appreciate – Old Country habits die hard – plus they stick to themselves and don't interfere. A place like this, you don't want people poking at you with questions about this or that. You come for a reason, or like me, you get sent, and nobody wants to talk about that.

It's Nil Sorski's Eve – he's the patron saint of the *skit* at the end of the village. The monks came from the big monastery at Beloozero years ago and though there's only eleven left, they own a lot of land, which is bizarre considering their patron was known as Nil the Non-Possessor and got into trouble for claiming all monks should be poor. They also make a radish liqueur that men have killed for, and on the Eve of Nil Sorski those who've done them well during the past twelve months each get a couple of bottles. It's blackmail, obviously, but it works, and for those who get given, it's the biggest night of the year.

Bernard had to re-sump their cess-pit back in June when the thaw threatened to sink their radish-plots and the entire crop along with it. One big favour deserves another, and we've got a crate of the stuff and beggars have been hammering at the door all day. Bernard took precautions and strengthened the bolts whilst I dug the dirt up under the fire – the only place the earth's loose – and buried most of the cache for later use. We've also put several in the eaves for the coming week, though out of drunken reach in case we get thirstier tonight than we ought, or visitors get violent.

In honour of Nil Sorski the Non-Possessor we hand over our goods to each other, a gesture of great trust in this climate of cold and starvation. Bernard has given me a bottle containing my two ears. I am so touched that I almost weep. He must have fought the wild dogs to get them, and beaten off that blasted woman who makes unguents out of anything she can get her hands on. Human parts are especially powerful, or so she tells anyone that will listen. When someone goes off into the forest to hunt elk or bear, they always take vodka to keep them warmed up. And she's always there when they return in case they got too drunk and fell asleep in the snow and got frostbite. She'll go round after them scraping up the blackened bits the second they've fallen off. Some would say that it's a harmless hobby, and that's she's only cleaning up what others don't want, but when she tries to sell you some disgusting black-green poultice, you have to wonder how many hunters' fingers and toes have gone into the mix.

It's with such thoughts in mind that I gaze gratefully at my bottled ears. The lump in my throat stops me speaking, so I pat Bernard on the back and, wobbling to my feet with the aid of a stick, go to get my gift for him. I take my special jar from below my bed and hand it over. It is half-filled with sugar gems the size of gooseberries. They are webbed all over with gold-leaf and coloured the brightest crocus yellow you've ever seen. The sherbet fizz and tang of lemon hide the treasure within – a sunflower seed carved in the profile of the Emperor, the Blessed Bonaparte. We take one each and suck it with reverence, removing the seed and laying it carefully to dry upon the hearth. Time was, we had to swallow them so our allegiance would remain unknown, but nobody cares, not now, not here. Still, it's a secret pleasure we'll not share with anyone else. They remind us of our glory days when we were young and strong.

For over fifteen years I've carried that jar of lozenges, a talisman of my faith and my adopted country. I thought The Corsican would save Europe; I spied for him at Austerlitz, paraded my Prussian papers, fought for the Austrians, allied myself to Alexander, fed false information to the Russian generals. We went from strength to strength. I fought with Bonaparte through Krasnoi and Smolensk and then, at Borodino, we hatched a plan and once again I was enlisted as a spy. I borrowed the uniform of a deceased officer and withdrew with the defeated Russian troops. I would glean what intelligence I could about what Commander-in-Chief Kutusov planned to do next. I would sow dissent and dis-ease amongst the ranks, and then I would desert and join my own army back on the banks of the Niemen. If I hadn't got accidentally shot by a boy who'd got head-fever and gone mad, all would have been well. However, when Bernard dragged me onto the hospital cart and I declared myself Brigade Leader Lyubivich number 53024, my rank was hotly disputed by a fellow patient who claimed to know that I was no such thing. It was a bad moment, and was only resolved when I punched the patient hard in the head, whereupon he died. A court-martial followed, with the result that I was convicted for stealing a senior officer's uniform – apparently my fellow patient would have been dead within the week even without my intervention, so the murder charge was dropped. I chose exile over imprisonment and, as Bernard frequently reminds me, we should count ourselves lucky that the military were in such disarray and the court proceedings shabby and unenthusiastic, or we would certainly have been discovered as the spies we were. He's right, of course; he's always been the better man than me.

I hand him over the jar. It was the one thing, apart from Bernard, that I was allowed to take with me into exile. Just a bag of lemons-drops, the Russians were told, to help me with the cold. Had they known what they really were – symbol of Empire and their defeat – I'd have been long buried, my head somewhere separate from my feet.

Bernard cradles the jar upon his knees, his eyes shining in their reflected glow. We pour another drink and clink our glasses, toast our faith and freedom. I tell him again to be careful with those sweets – only one every now and then. The startling colour comes from Acid of Picric, and though stunning to see and marvellous to taste, it has the slight disadvantage of being poisonous. More so than arsenic, I am told, and I add the story – possibly apocryphal – of Ludwig, King of Bavaria, who almost killed his entire court by creating confectionery canaries in cages of spun sugar. These replaced the real ones, two hours earlier singing their heads off and now spitted arse-to-beak upon the fire. He might have been mad, but one doubts that there was murder on his mind. Although, of course, it could have been the chef. They could make you eat yesterday's stockings if they're good enough at their job; make the worst ingredients taste good. One can imagine a building up of bitterness if they're not appreciated for what they do. A bit like spies. Although one assumes that most cooks don't become murderers.

I, on the other hand, have already removed a small handful of my golden sweets. I have placed them in a leather pouch and posted them through the door of Patrovich Davidov. He is a mean and greedy man who drinks two cups of vodka before breakfast, and who lost his wife to a man who digs holes for a living. Any kind of hole will do, and hard work though it is to dig in our soil, it's hardly the height of social climbing. And yet this Patrovich Davidov, the sole accuser at my trial, was believed above me because he works in the courthouse and I only graft in the factory. What use would I have for Councillor Rostov's pocket watch, Bernard (as my defence lawyer) demanded of the judge? We all know it stops in the autumn and doesn't start again till spring. That I *did* have a use for it is none of anyone's business but my own. Its innards made a fine pair of earrings for Valda – whose services, as even Davidov knows, don't come cheap.

Ah well. What's done is done. Bernard has poured me another drink and the fire is finally warming my bones. I can hardly hear the constant beggars battering at the door; shortly we will have to let them in before they get out the ice-picks. And, thanks to Bernard, my ears are safe upon the shelf. I am told that my hearing will recover – there's quite a few round about who've had the thieves' verdict passed upon them – so once again I will have the pleasure of hearing the swans fly low in spring, and pretend to understand Bernard's obscure jokes. Valda is used to those of us lacking in such appendages and anyway, she says that she means to retire. I have saved enough silver to fashion a ring, and thank God once again for His blessing. God bless France, which I once believed would give the world the liberty and equality it still needs. God bless Bernard for being a sage friend and saver of ears. God bless Napoleon and those who made gilded sherbets in his image. God Bless St Sorski and all the seraphim for this night of gifts. And Davidov will find his, I have no doubt; and being a greedy man and without friends or wife, he will no doubt consume the entire golden hoard himself and gain his just desserts. Thank you, Rostov, for your watch. Because of you I have lost my ears, but Valda has a fine present for her retirement, most of which I do not doubt she will spend with me. And, like the walrus, I will do most of my listening on the inside.

Always Keep Your Shovel Sharp

*S*ecrets

Odo's got his father's eel-dish out. It fits three spiralled eels and a gallon of marinade. He didn't use it much. Preferred to slice and salt them on a spit, smoke them over an apple-wood fire. He was particular about the apple-wood; nothing else would do.

Says Odo

That's not what's in the dish today, though. What's in it today is entirely mine, hidden in a crust for almost fifteen years. You'd think that crust would've dissolved by now, being only wheat-flour and water, but it was cooked real slow and dried over days and that makes it hard as stone. And there it's been all this time, sitting on a shelf in the pantry. It's what we've fought over, my brother and I. He swore I had it, I swore I didn't and he never found it though he looked. A thousand times he's been in and searched this place. When he thinks I'm out, it's in he creeps, shifts the sacks in the cellar, rummages under rain barrels, prises up the bricks around the hearth or the stones along the paths.

He used to scream and shout, hours at a time, swearing like a shovel-load of shit. I just sat and smoked or went to a neighbour's for a bottle. He'd be gone when I got back.

And here it is, and I had it all along, and he was right. Lucky for me that he's dead now, and at last it's time to take the eel-pan out the pantry and break the crust.

Why, Odo, why?

It's a bad business when the barley fails and the river water-logs the fields: rows of fodder-crop soldiers rotting feet-first, backs that tire and break, lay their heads upon the water until the last one's drowned, and when the river returns to its banks there's nothing left but sodden stalks and slime.

It was the worst winter anyone remembered: the bread rough and hard with straw and bark, the pea-flour staining it green. The mould got in and sent a few of us mad, laughing like banshees, licking up the dirt, or throwing themselves off the cliffs believing they could fly. Of course they couldn't, and their bodies fed the seagulls as the village fell away into the sea.

Of all of us, only one man was happy, and it was odd to see Odo Fletcher smile so hard the cracks at the side of his mouth began to bleed. It seemed his brother had gone off the cliff with the others and at last, after fifteen years, the family feud that had blighted their lives and ours had finally come to an end.

'It's like lying awake at night,' says Odo, 'listening to the water shnoozzle up the beach and down, up and down, up and down, combing through the sand, sucking at the silt, here and there, back and forth amongst the pebbles.' It was peace and calm, said Odo, after a day of noise and shouting and vile abuse. It was a dog sleeping on the rug and a pot of beans and bacon by the fire. Of course by then we had no beans and bacon, and every last dog was eaten right down to its tail. Still, said Odo Fletcher, that's how it felt to walk at last around his house and land in peace. We'd have been glad for him if we'd cared, but by then we were busy chewing the leather buttons off our shirts or boiling up roots for tea or searching every tree in the wood for skin-thin squirrels or setting traps for the old, sick badgers that hadn't run off or been eaten by the foxes, who perversely were fatter than they had ever been.

When everything was over and we'd put some weight back on our creaking bones and tallied up the ones who'd died and scratched their names on a big stone slab we'd dragged out of the quarry; when everything was rested again, and we'd patched our houses, replaced the thatch we'd taken down and boiled into stew, when we'd got lucky in the woods and caught us a boar for spitting, when all that was done and the winter finally went and we had time to sit a little and drink a little beer, that was when we sat around and thought about Odo Fletcher and his brother and all that had happened all those many years ago. And what had really pushed his brother over the cliff.

When mothers die young & bad women take their places

Their ma had died before she hit twenty, leaving Odo and Arnold and their old stick of a dad behind. He was twice her age, hard and curled as briar wood and made his boys work hard as him, which was harder than most of us put together. They had the best farm going and every stone of every wall was right in place and strong, and every hedge was layered so close to the ground you couldn't slide a slow-worm through the gaps. There wasn't much of an age between those brothers, and when the old man died they put him under the cabbage patch to make his last use and carried on just as before. They weren't bad looking boys, and what with the way they worked they were taut and tanned, lean as hazel switches, and of course they had land and money. We weren't short of girls in our village, and my own two had tried their best, but Odo and Arnold were never much bothered bar the odd huff and giggle behind the big barn at New Year's, and that was after cider enough to fell an ox. There's no denying it, we'd none of us have minded getting our hands on that farm and our girls did their damndest, but those brothers would have none of it. And that was how it went for a while and a while. Until the new tack-worker came and set up shop with his family.

The trouble caused by girls reading books

The daughter wasn't pretty, but she had a something about the way she moved and laughed, and she used to sit on the church steps on summer evenings, a book open on her lap. Soon enough she was reading out stories to a knot and snot of kids, and by and by we all fell into it, and we'd gather there on a night after work and she'd light a lamp and read us tales of places far away.

And after a while, Odo and Arnold started coming by and it wasn't long after that that she started going up to their place. And it wasn't long after that that Arnold shifted all his gear and moved permanent into the summer cottage by the lake, and they'd built a big stone dyke all down the centre of their father's land and she'd be coming and going between the two of them. Well, that sort of situation can't go on for long and the tack-man told her to take her pick. She puzzled a week or two and then the bans were read and Arnold and the girl decided to be wed in the spring.

We never saw much of Odo after that; he just stayed on his side of the dyke and carried on digging and hoeing and planting and weeding and smoking and wattling and shearing and fattening his pigs for the winter.

Get that shovel

And then the girl disappeared. Or at least, part of her did. We found the rest out by the pier on the lake. It had been cold and the frost had tacked her to the boat-post, her blue dress stiff and rimed with ice, the blanket round her shoulders thick and wet. Her fingers were white as whey and the book they held was still open, though the page had soaked through and was covered with a sprinkle of snow so you couldn't see any of the words. And there we found her the morning after her dad had shouted out the village that she'd not come home. It was her all right, with the dress and the book and those pale fingers, but we never saw her face again.

And neither did Arnold, though he'd looked all those years. Maybe that was why he finally went over the cliff, because he'd looked every place else. He'd dredged the lake as far as he could, he'd been through the woods, he'd knocked down walls and turned over boulders. He'd stood outside his brother's and shouted and pleaded and cried and cursed until the inside of his throat began to bleed. But he never did find her head.

Of course, we wondered about Odo and how perhaps he

hadn't taken things quite as well as it seemed. But what could we do? We buried the bits that were left and the tack-man and his family soon moved on and left us pretty much as we had been before. And the years came and went until that time when the harvest drowned in the floods and we had the worst winter anyone remembered. That was the winter Arnold went over the cliff and Odo remembered how to smile.

What's cooking, Odo?

Odo remembers the way her lips moved when she was reading, her dark eyes lowered, the top of her head shining in the light of the lamp. It was how he always thought of her, and he hoped she hadn't minded the dark for all these years. He hadn't meant to do what he did that day he'd gone up to the lake, but there he'd gone, to dig out the eel-run which had got all silted and grown-over since summer. He'd wanted to see the big blue of the lake as the sun sank low behind the clouds, see the water blush and bleed, take the boat out slow and certain, drop a line for the night-time fish. And then there she was, leaning up against the boat-post, legs curled up underneath her, a blanket round her shoulders. She had a book open on her lap but she wasn't reading; her eyes were open, gazing towards the summer house which was soon to be her home and her lips were slightly parted like it was her who was humming soft and low, and not the grebes calling out over the lake. He'd stood by the boathouse, watching her, his breath caught in his throat, and then a trout jumped up and sent silver ripples like a gift towards him, and he'd known in that moment that the summer house would never be her home and that those eyes would never read another word and those lips would never tell another tale and he had flung himself across the shingle until he stood in front of her sending the shovel singing through the air, hammering it home till it bit the hard wood behind her neck. She had drawn a line down the middle of his life and now he would draw one down hers. He tucked the best of her under his arm, washed the shovel in the lake, and went home.

Always Keep Your Shovel Sharp

Sixteen years alive, only fifteen dead

Hard winter, hard times for the rest of us, but for Odo things couldn't have been better. With his brother gone it was time again to see those lips, look at the lamplight linger on her hair. He put the eel-pan on the table and lifted off the lid. He picked up the small hammer and began very gently to tap-tap-tap away the crust.

As for me...

Well, Arnold's gone as you know, and not so long ago, Odo too went over that cliff. Might've been the winter taking its toll, or maybe he missed his brother even though they'd feuded all those years. Who knows? He said nothing to no-one. Maybe he just slipped. It could've been like that, anyway. There was a big pie broken open on his table, and all the insides eaten out, though not a plate or fork in sight. But Odo was a tidy man; maybe he washed and dried them before taking himself out for a walk. We could see his steps going through the snow, up to the boat-house. We found his shovel leaning against the post and then his footsteps peeled away and headed straight for where the cliff is highest and falls away into the sea. It looked like he'd stood there a while, maybe looking out to where the sun sometimes glows green as it melts into the sea. Funny thing was, we found a scrap of paper in the drawer of his kitchen table covered with his scrawl. Left everything he owned to that old tack-man. 'Course no-one knew where he was or even where he'd gone, so we threw it on the fire, and each took a little bit of this and a little bit of that which is the way things have always been. I've got the plot of land on the lake-shore leading up to the cottage, the old dresser-drawers and his dad's eel-pan. I always liked that eel-pan; good for brawn – takes a whole pig's head if you can cram it in. Took a bit of cleaning; don't think Odo can have used it for years. That crust was hard as rock. Still, I think of him sometimes when I take the eel-pan out the pantry, or stand by the boat-house, watching the sun slide slowly towards the lake.

I had to dig out the old boat-post last year and just by it found a skull. Right where the tack-man's girl had been found. Right where Odo had left his shovel before going off the cliff. I didn't tell no-one now that it's all so long ago, just picked the thing up and heaved it far as I could into the water. I'd always wondered what happened to her head, because I knew I hadn't taken it. I'd left her right where she was after I'd popped her neck bones with my dog-chain. Only took a few seconds – you learn a few things when you've lived as long as me. Like that people always get what's coming to them and they shouldn't take what they don't deserve. We put up with Odo and Arnold forever, but land is land and was a long time coming. I just helped things along is all, which is the privilege of the old and wise. I'll enjoy my little piece of land and my boat-post and my chest of drawers and every now and then I'll catch a few eels and take out my pan from the pantry.

Thanks, Odo.

Always said you should enjoy things while you can.

Hinklemann Hits the Cellar

L ife was pretty good for me in those days, having cornered the market in Ancient Eggs and Tabby-stones. One good week would follow another.

One particular morning I was leaning back in my chair sated, the remnants of my boiled-egg breakfast piled neatly upon my plate, and Millia, my housemaid, hovering with a tray of fresh coffee – when we both heard an almighty commotion in the cellar. I tore the napkin from my chin and raced to the stairs. Millia was two steps behind, her tray abandoned, her hands holding her skirts so she would not fall. We clattered down the treads, catching slippers on the risers, forgetting to light a candle to see our way. We didn't need to. When we reached the bottom and opened the door, the whole room glowed a ghastly green, and a few eggs bobbed here and there. The noxious smell made me at once regret ridding myself of the napkin, and my hand flew to cover my nose. Behind me, Millia bumped into my back, then made a sort of screech and fled away up the steps to call the doctor. I doubted there was much a doctor could do, but I supposed it was worth a try. There was plenty I'd have to say to the fellow who was floating face-down on my cellar floor, surround by the up-turned egg-bath and several broken barrels of tabby-stones and maturing *Angs*. However, I didn't doubt for a moment that the man was dead. He was naked, a blue island in a chemical sea, the shipwreck of my misfortune.

We are, you see, a town devoted to death and dying. A city within a necropolis, our walls surrounded by the gardens of the dead. We try to pretty them up, of course, and our aspiring gardeners weave roses into tumbrels, clip hedges into birds, build fountains which sparkle water over islands of mossy stones, ponds which drink in the rain, pooling blue and cool between the headstones, drawing it through streams, trickling silver bracelets through the cemeteries. But there are no fish in the pools. Nothing lives in them. The waters are steeped with the exudations of decay. At night come the hedgehogs to eat the maggots of the flies which cluster at the edges of the streams.

We are ruled by church and prison. Everyday another coach-load of apostates and murderers comes trundling across the countryside through our vineyards and crop-fields, down the terraces of plums and cherries, through our graveyards, past the gibbets and rood-stones, through the gates below the tolling bell and on through the cobbled streets to incarceration, torture and death. Most come to us in silence, their cloaks drawn tight around their skinny bodies, eyes pulled close into their brows. Who wanted to look over our pretty gardens and know there was no escape? If you came into Lubbaylich like that, there was only one way to leave.

Despite our reputation and the subtle smell of sweet decay which hung over our towers and houses, threading early-morning mist along our streets and lanes, as a town we thrived. Naturally, there were rope-makers and embalmers, undertakers and grave-diggers by the dozen. Our Mortuary Memorabilia was world famous. We made caskets and lockets, rings and plaques and portraits, cutlery and tableware, chairs and furniture, out of all sorts of things.

'Give us anything and we'll find the bones in it,' was our motto. We could turn anything, anything at all into *Memento Mori*. We made a four-poster for the Saxon Duke using the bones of his executed wife. We made a drinking tankard from a man's skull. We paid the prisoners a penny an inch for their hair and wove it into wigs. They handed their earnings over to the priest for a prayer, or to the executioner for a quick passing. We made candlesticks from femurs, chandeliers of ribs, turned knuckles into inkstands. We were renowned for our craftsmanship, our gold-chasers, our gardeners. We were visited by the finest surgeons and anatomists. We had many a famous artist and sculptor study within our walls, and the streets were awash with musicians scribbling down masses and requiems which it seems they just plucked from the air.

And so to my own occupation, until I found that corpse in

15

my cellar. I first soak my eggs in water-glass: my own recipe, viscous and transparent, like the inside of an ox's eyeball. The shells have a fine craquelure, to be enhanced by a tannin dye. Then the eggs go into vinegar to soften them up, so they can be squeezed through the neck of a bottle. I load them onto my cart and take them to the market in Hümpfelture Platz and flog them for a silver coin apiece. They are the talk of the court in Lubbaylich, and everyone must have one! I always take care to drop a drift of rumours about the place, wafting here and there like autumn leaves. *These ancient eggs will cure diseases, they alleviate the pains of childbirth and tuberculosis, invigorate the impotent, ease the madness of syphilis and the agony of gout.* They go well with my previous best-seller, a tabby-stone set with a gold clasp and chain, laid on a bed of silk. These ward off evil airs and night-terrors, the ghosts of the damned, the hungry spectres who prowl the streets at night.

I doubt I could have made such stories stick in some place more sophisticated – Vienna, say, or Salzburg – but here in Lubbaylich people are ready to believe anything, as you will see.

'Well, what the blazes was a notorious heretic like Hans Hinklemann doing in my cellar?'

I am having a somewhat heated discussion with Herr Hochwürden Doktor Villbergen, who is a cross between a military policeman and a Jesuit sniffer dog. He is spreading his long fingers about my table, where they look uncommonly like frogs' legs.

'That, my dear Herr Tessler, is what we are trying to find out. Did you hear nothing, nothing at all during the night?'

Exasperated, I fling my coffee spoon across the table where it hits the milk jug with an annoyingly undramatic plink.

'I have told you at least three times, Doktor, that neither I nor my housemaid heard anything. I sleep on the middle floor and Millia in the attic, so it is unlikely that either of us would have been wakened by some stealthy sneakit breaking in. And if the egg-bath and barrels were carefully upturned, the ensuing flood would have muffled any sound. The first we heard was an almighty crash this morning, which one presumes was my chemical cupboard at last breaking from its wall-supports and capsizing into the general mêlée. That would also account for the unearthly glow down there. My white phosphorous – which I went to considerable pains and expense to procure – has started to oxidise. It is somewhat poisonous, so I would advise your minions to take a little care when removing your heathen carcass.'

I knew I sounded peevish, but really, it had been a rather trying morning. In addition to the almost total loss of my saleable stock and several months' worth of supplies, I was now being subjected to an interrogation, as if I would be so ridiculously dim-witted as to murder a complete stranger in my own cellar! Furthermore, Villbergen has imported a posse of monks to sing prayers over the deceased and the noise is beginning to get on my nerves.

'Herr Tessler.' Villbergen raises his hand and closes his eyes in order to pre-empt another interruption. 'I am not inclined to believe that you had anything to do with the ante-mortem disposition of the man in your cellar. It seems he escaped the northerly prison last night with the aid of several sympathetic guards, who have since been despatched to eternity.'

He pauses to allow the casualness of death sink in.

'The man was a blasphemer, an idolater and a troublemaker. He has been responsible for any number of riots not only in Vienna but as far north as Frankfurt. It seems he denies Mother Church any role in his relationship with the Saviour whom he regards as a Brother in that, and I quote, *'we are all the sons and daughters of Creation and of God who is the Father of Creation.'*

'Would that not make us God's grandchildren?' It is an idle comment which I throw in without thinking.

'Therein lies the core of blasphemy,' says the good Villbergen. 'It implies a carnal relationship within the deific ménage, and requires a female embodiment of Glory.'

I am shaking my head. Most of us here in Lubbaylich tread the religious path rather lightly. Perhaps we are a little too familiar with death to allow it to worry us overmuch.

'Ho hum,' we are as like to say as not: 'one day that will be me.'

Which is just about the extent of our theological pre-occupations.

'So if he went to all the trouble to escape, how the jiggery did he end up murdered in my cellar?'

The priest moves his fingers across the tablecloth, tracing an arc. 'There seems no logic in it. And yet, my dear Herr Tessler, logic there always is.'

So much for Church and Town working together. As usual, the church commanded and the town complied. The body of my mysterious visitor was carried out of my back door, still dripping, and attached to the tail-end of a horse. From there, it was dragged through the streets bouncing and pummelling itself into a darker shade of blue and was then ceremonially hung up by the neck. For three days the blue body of the heretic Hinklemann swung upon the gibbet while we waited for the Duke and his entourage to arrive. It was a solemn affair, with visiting dignitaries and us townspeople crowding round (we were obliged to swell the numbers). Also present was a whole horde of Hinklemann heretics who were forced to kneel in a circle around the rood-stone whilst their leader was de-limbed, gutted, quartered and thrown to the four corners of the earth. It was no wonder our town smelt like an abattoir at times, but our flesh-toters were quick on the trail, gleaning what they could to sell back to relatives or for fertilizer cakes – whatever turned the most profit. Out came the jugglers and the dancers, and drink poured from the taverns like water. The heretic audience learned the error of their ways and coughed up a confession before being separated from their heads. Those who refused to recant were despatched more painfully by fire, their cursed ashes staining our Sunday cloaks.

Naturally I got no compensation for my losses despite several petitions to the Burgermeister and a week wasted grovelling at court.

Nor did I find out what the man was doing in my cellar. It was posited that, having escaped, he met with a helper to arrange a disguise, for convenience at the back of my house, which is near the Northern Gate. Said friend took him to my cellar where he divested himself of clothes; whereupon friend turned traitor and despatched him. Perhaps he had a knife, but seeing the situation, chose to entertain us with a riddle. There were no marks on Hinklemann and I was sure he had drowned. Not in the river, but in *my* cellar, in *my* glass-water. If I was not convinced of this at first, I was certain of it several months later.

The flesh-toters had sold the Hinklemann remains to his followers, who had infiltrated the city to bear witness to his martyrdom. They put him in a casket and buried him in one of the more distant vaults. When the ruse was discovered, Hochwürden Villbergen sent men to dig up the casket and bring it to the central Platz – which was a mistake, in my opinion, if anyone had asked. The idea was to chuck the casket on a fire, but when the casket was opened, Herr Hinklemann's face smiled out in perfect preservation and his body, though in bits, was intact. It was said there was a smell of violets. The obligatory riot ensued and was bloodily put down. Too late, for Herr Hinklemann had been spirited away to Vienna and Holy Grace. Emboldened, his followers rose up and were not to be put down. Herr Hochwürden Doktor Villbergen, having been demoted to a bishopric in Vienna for allowing such a debacle, was dragged from his house and set on fire in his own back yard. Lucky for him, the mob fled without seeing the end of the show, and he managed to propel himself into his ornamental pond. His hair never grew back and his fine long fingers were permanently fused, but he lived to curse again the name of Hinklemann.

And so, that is my part in my country's history. Not that many people know about it, despite my constantly telling them: 'It was the glass-water – the special fluid I use to preserve my eggs. It embalmed the heretic inside and out when he sucked it up in my cellar!'

No-one listens, and my eggs have rather gone out of fashion.

Hinklemann Hits the Cellar

The Hinklemann episode inspired other ideas: I paid prisoners for fingers and toes and gave them the egg treatment. And, behold, they became relics from Jerusalem from this saint or that ... until I was arrested for simony and thrown into jail. I was only there a week, but that was long enough. It gives you a sense of solidarity, being cooped up with so many condemned souls, fearing to be mistaken for one of them. My neck is more precious to me now, and I no longer trouble the condemned for miscellaneous body parts. There are plenty that still do, so maybe I am just being sentimental. Whatever, I have developed a new line.

Now I sell toys to the visiting gentry – small automata which show a man on the scaffold being hung. You wind the thing up and the trap-door drops open, and down goes the man, eyes blinking, mouth opening and closing like a beached fish. I even have one model who kicks off his boots and sticks out his tongue. It is very effective and sells well.

And a man must needs make his living.

Stepping on Seals

You can see a long way from the mizzen mast, especially when you've been strung up by your heels and have nothing better to do but blow in the wind and concentrate on the view. After a while, my vision blurs with the weight of draining blood and my head feels like the butt-end of a pear. I'll have passed out in a few minutes but I've just time to make out the edges of Saari-Ma – the island country where I was born and where boulders rise like ruined castles from woodland thickets, black against the green of the Rigan Gulf.

'Pendulosis,' observes the ship's doctor, having untangled me from the rigging. 'See here: the swollen and engorged face, the slight red sheen to the sweat; and again here,' he points the place out to his pupil, a small boy scared of the sea, 'the feet and ankles have shrunk from lack of lymph and blood. This explains how they slipped their knots and released their bottom-heavy burden to the ground. It is not dissimilar to the way some fruit depends then detaches from its stem. Mulberries come immediately to mind, possibly because of the similarity of facial colouring in our patient here. Watch out!'

There is a second whoosh of plummeting pendulosis as another body descends into the rigging net.

Me and Ulli Rueland are jammed together on the doctor's operating table. Next to us is his trolley of scalpels, clamps and knives. It's the first thing I see when finally I break the crust of salt and clotted blood and open my eyes: the glint of moonlight on metal, Ulli's profile against the white of the wall, the open crevasse of his mouth, the flattened crag of his four times-broken nose. I say four, but it may be more. I only know of the times when he was with me: the first when we'd swum out to collect eggs on Bird Shit Island and he'd gone headfirst down a cliff. Luckily the cliffs are small on Linussitamaa and the bag of eggs he was carrying broke his fall. The second time was when we'd started a partnership in roof-reeding. We never lasted a season – I sliced off three fingers while scything reeds and Ulli kept sliding off the roofs. The last two times his host broke it himself. Ever since the roof-reeding disaster, job-hunting had been tough and money short. Thinking hard of our future demanded heavy drinking, which resulted in many schemes, most of which were outrageous in their idiocy. We could import monkeys from Gibraltar and train them to collect eggs, weave ready-made reed-mats for roofs, roll cigarettes for amputees. We could chisel out some of the great boulders on the islands and sell them as houses to Russian exiles, or carve them into fantastic faces, invite the monarchy to visit them, start a lucrative European craze: everyone knows those mainland Europeans are crazy. We could fill in the meteorite craters on Ösel-Saaremaa and make inland lakes, stock them with gudgeon and grayling, those strange fish that taste of cucumbers that they like so much in Sweden. We spent hours discussing these detailed plans and several times came to blows, me using my head instead of my fists, of which I only had one after the reed-scything incident. Perhaps we should've trained monkeys to use the scythes and saved me a lot of bother and one hand.

It was our latest scheme that had ended with us head-down in the rigging of the Rigan Lady and now, side by side on the doctor's slab, waiting to have our kneecaps hammered back into place.

'Interesting side-effect of pendulosis,' says the doctor tugging at his beard, his pupil concentrating hard, hoping to stay below decks, regretting ever having signed up to sea, 'the steadily increasing density of body fluids to the lower parts of the upside-down body, particularly the chest cavity and cerebrum, seems to have loosened the tendons around the patella and popped the knee right off its knuckle.'

He puts a leather strop in my mouth and tells me to put my tongue to one side and get ready to bite. We've waited a while for the vodka to kick in, but I can feel myself shrinking in my skin for fear and sweat drips from my head and hands. Ulli has the better of it, being unconscious, and hardly flinches when the hammer cracks the bones back into place. Unfortunately

I couldn't be more awake and the doctor refuses me more alcohol telling me it should be kept for emergencies. I demand to know what greater emergency there could be than this and the doctor laughs out loud and turns to select his hammer.

'When a man's had his arm half bitten off by a seal or peed in the path of a swordfish, or he's swallowed a hook and his gullet needs shoving back down his throat, or he's fallen on the blubber saw and needs his top sewn back to his bottom. That, my lad, would be a case for more alcohol; for you though, it's the strap.'

Back in the brig which doubles as the gutting hold, rubbing our sore knees and it's back on the bean-and-barley soup. They deliberately use the old fish-soak water, so we're thirsty as hell again and the stink makes us throw up what we've managed to get down.

'What the hell are we doing here?' I demand of Ulli.

'It was your bloody idea,' he replies, chucking up the last of his soup.

'My idea to go sealing,' I'm yelling right in his face: 'your idea to desert.'

Within minutes we're rolling into barrels and throwing punches and Ulli gets his nose broken all over again.

'We've got to think of something better,' we're both agreed. We've calmed down and he hands me a soggy cigarette. It tastes of rotting fish, and the flint is too wet to spark so we have to chew the tobacco instead, paper and all because it's got stuck together.

'No monkeys,' I say quietly and the words die on my lips.

'I've heard you can make a canoe from inflated seal-stomachs.' Ulli catches my eye, doesn't bother going on. We talk and talk until the moon shines down through the planking, sets the place alight with silver scales. At dog-leg watch we're wakened by the creak of the hatch. A flask comes flying down through the darkness and we hear shoes sighing over the boards as our helper creeps back to the wheel.

'Eric,' I say.

'Eric,' says Ulli.

We pass the flask back and forth; Ulli rubs some on his nose to ease the pain. I don't begrudge him. The vodka's been peppered to warm our bones through the night. Winter ice will soon crack across the water, whisper its way over the sands of the bay, make bridges between the islands, link lands lost to each other all the long summer months. And then, when the flask is almost emptied, we have a truly marvellous idea...

'Shit,' says Ulli, and I cannot disagree. We're lying side by side on the doctor's slab, our knuckles once again separated from our knees.

'I really thought it would work that time,' I nod. My head feels like a coconut drained of milk and my mouth is dry as the desert.

'Monkeys,' I croak.

'Next time,' says Ulli, and we watch the moonlight cracking the white walls.

'I blame Eric,' says Ulli, and I echo his name, thinking of Eric milk-pale under the blue-iced glaze of the sea.

Upstairs in his study, the Skipper spins his globe. There's a candle inside which flickers through Russia and the Arctic and the Australian archipelago. Stops on the Tasmanian Straits.

'What were they thinking?' He talks to the cat, thick as marmalade, purring on his knee. 'And poor Eric. We all knew he hated the sea, but this... Well, who'd have thought.'

He leaned over his desk, picked up his pen and carried on writing his report:

> *'To the Master at Arms of Kuivastu Harbour, Muhu Island, Mother Port of the Sealing Ship, The Rigan Lady.*
>
> *We regret to inform you of the loss of one of our crew, Eric Musthaagen, and the imprisonment of two others, Ulli Rueland and Woolgar Rupke. This follows an ill-advised attempt to desert whilst the Rigan Lady was at anchor off the Prangli Islands in the Finnish Gulf. The*

*conspirators, who had already been apprehended for
various felonies whilst on board, apparently convinced
or coerced Mr Musthaagen, who was on watch at the
time, to join them. Their plan appears to have been to
reach the lighthouse on Keri Island and then steal the
Keeper's boat and head for the mainland. To achieve
this, they launched themselves into the water using
empty barrels as rafts, not realising that the sea-surface
hereabouts had already begun its winter freeze, and
although no obstacle to a sealing ship, the ice caused
considerable drag on their barrels. The remaining crew
were wakened by the alarmed shouts of the deserters
as their barrels jammed and pitched them into the
water. We were able to effect the rescue of two of them,
but Mr Musthaagen had been too long in the water
to resuscitate. We suggest the surviving deserters be
charged with being the cause of his death.'*

Ulli and Woolgar, due to popular demand, are hanging once
again from the mast. The Skipper has stayed in his cabin,
pretending not to know what is going on. Everyone liked Eric,
who would have been fourteen next week. He'd been a sort
of mascot; kind, if not exactly bright, considered lucky by the
crew, particularly because he was so afraid of the water, as
every good sailor is, though he'd never admit it. The Skipper
can hear the doctor two cabins down bashing his instruments
about, selecting the largest hammers he can find. Behind the
boat, a line of severed seal heads bob up on the broken ice,
thrown out at intervals by the gutting crew. They are meant
as a threat to the prisoners, who would have been hung right
way up if the first mate hadn't intervened. The Captain sighs
and puts the report away in his pocket. The cat grumps off his
knee, annoyed at being disturbed.

I can see across the ice-bound wastes to Saari-ma where I was
born, and then the wind swings me the other way. I see the
seal-head stepping-stones reaching toward Finland and wonder
if they'd've worked as well as the barrels. Better, probably. The

latest head hits the freezing water with a thump. It sinks slightly then comes up whiskers first, glaring at me, baring its teeth. For a dreadful moment I think I see Eric's face and then I'm falling again, and this time the rigging gives way when I land on it and I hit the planking of the deck with an awful crunch. I see the doctor advance towards me and know with absolute certainty that there's no alcohol for Woolgar this time, none at all. I think of Eric, who won't be passing vodka to us in the brig tonight to ease our sore knees and throats. I think of Ulli and make a silent vow: let him break his own nose from now on, because I'm done. There's bad and there's worse, and I'm going no further. Maybe I'll travel, go to Gibraltar. Maybe there's something to this monkey thing after all. At least it's a plan, and it can't be as bad as this. I see the doctor smile as he selects his hammer, and obediently put my tongue to one side and turn my head away. Try and think of picking crowberries on a bright autumn morning, end up thinking of an axe splitting wood.

Thwack!

I try not to scream, but it's too much and before I know it, my tongue's gone back down my throat and I can't breathe. The doctor notices, sighs, pulls out my tongue with a pair of tongs, then he picks up the hammer again and snaps my second knee-bone in two.

'One down,' he says, and goes to his desk, sips at his warm vodka. Ulli's unconscious again, but the doctor can wait. He's a patient man.

The Dog at the Crossroads

'Jesus and Mary!'

Henry Dibblewitch skids backwards into the carefully-stacked peat-riddle, ends with his knees knocked out by the bank, sitting, breathing hard, watching the head he has decapitated rolling out from under his spade. Henry puts a hand to his chest, tries to calm himself, feels his heart slow and sink from its sudden leap. He leans forward, sees the spade still vibrating where it stuck in the peat, sees the head rolling to rest on its cheek. It is black as the bog from which it has come, tanned like hide, bristles still stubbling its chin, brows still gathered over half-closed eyes. Cold water has seeped through Henry's trousers and begun to gather in the cracks behind his knees. He puts a hand on the spade, eases himself up, pulls the spade free and uses its edge to poke first at the head and then at the bank from which it has come. A stump of neck pokes out where a seep of water clears the way around it, makes it look like it has been put there only yesterday.

But Henry Dibblewitch has a feeling it has been there a lot longer than that. About forty-two years, is his reckoning.

There's a dog at the crossroads, old and grey as the hanging-post, joists and joints creaking slightly in the wind. He lifts his head, scents the air, knows it's not to the right or straight on, but away to the left with the wind. The marsh-pools are cracked over with ice, the breath of mist rising cold as the morning, waking the water-rails who groan deep and soft within reedy nests. The track where the dog passes is rutted and thick with rust-coloured mud. The cart must have been this way: a snap-headed bolt lies where it fell as the wheels shook and shuddered, going too fast at the ground, lifting boards, straining axles, pulling at pins and nails and shoddy repairs. A snipe cuts across the track, disturbed by the dog, zig-zagging, kik-kakking, disappearing into fog-filled ditches where the peat has been lifted and the hard, tawny water seeps up from below.

The Dog at the Crossroads

It's a good place for bogs, but the dog doesn't know it. He just keeps right on as the dawn arches over him, darkened by the rising mist, hidden by the drizzling rain which falls unseen, unceasing, sinking into the marsh of the meadows, into the skin of his back, damping the manging fur. His master falls away into the bog two yards to the left and the dog does not know it. His master is lost to him forever and is disappearing from the world into cold earth, dark water.

Or he was, until the bog is drained away to feed the fields and leaves a thick black root drying out below the morning sun, and the old dog's master's head is lopped from his shoulders by Henry Dibblewitch's peat-cutting spade.

Gumbert Frye has a face like a lakeland sky, a sun chased by storm-clouds, a rime of ice staying unmelted between two hard dark hills. He's not bad; he's not good. He lives his life as his father lived before him. Sheep are the only thing. Raise a good flock, raise another from it, keep a few good dogs and what else does a man need? Nothing else, said Gumbert's father, nothing else. That's what a man did back then. What a man still does: keeps going like he's always done. What the old dog does still when he sniffs at the crossroads, takes the road to the left. What the old dog did when he died there, cold and stiff, still waiting, corpse getting older and thinner till someone kicked the leathery rib-sack into the ditch and let him go. Gumbert would have wept to see his old dog alone at that crossroads, his nose still sniffing to the south, still trying to pad his way along the old rutted path, still following that old decrepit wagon that had passed that way so many, many years before.

What to do? thinks Henry Dibblewitch. What now is there to do? He stands by his peat-rick, leaning on his spade, and wonders what now is left to do. He lights his pipe, he gazes at the evening sun glowing red and green in a sky which will bring rain in the morning. He's trying his best not to remember, but still he does.

Gumbert is bringing his sheep down from the hills. He's got

the pen ready, and in it the big black-horned tup. Time for breeding, he thinks, like his father before him. Tup's ready, and so are the ewes.

It's a big old fierce one, liable to escape, so he ties it up with strong rope, tethers it to the fence, gets it into the retaining yoke, a Y of hard wood hammered into the ground. He doesn't see it then, but the ram's old bones are brittle and he's broken his leg against the yoke, he screams like the devil but Gumbert is used to the noise and teeth of that old tup, thinks nothing of it. He shoves the old ram's head into the V of the Y and quickly threads an iron pin through the holes to hold it fast.

Which is just what Henry Dibblewitch did to Gumbert that night he found him out back of the sheep-shed, hobbling Henry's very own ram, his new Hardwick which had cost him four good heifers and a half-year's supply of first-cut hay. He'd hammered that yoke so hard into the ground, a lightning strike wouldn't have moved it. He'd fixed that pin with double cleats so Gumbert's hands couldn't strain behind his back and slide it out. He'd left him out there in the paddock shouting and pleading, saying what about just a bit of a loan? Just a few goes at the ewes? His own one had broken a leg and was useless. He'd not time to go get another – no time, and no money. What was he to do? His ewes were all ready. You know how it is, Henry: them sheep just can't wait. Henry! he'd shouted. Henry! he'd pleaded.

Henry had gone back in to his dinner, but couldn't eat the turnip mash and cutlets lying cold upon his plate. He'd turned down the lamp so the wick only just glowed; he'd put on his slippers and sat smoking by the fire, watching the moon rise over the hill, watching the ice-crystals sparkle on the window, listening to Gumbert kicking and straining, bucking like an old ram that's waiting to be drenched or like that young collie that had took to fitting every time he come down off the hill with the sheep. He'd had to shoot that dog in the end, and it still made his throat tight to think on it.

Henry had waited till the fight had gone out of Gumbert

before going out to release him. Which was when he found it wasn't just the fight, but the life of him that had gone too. He was cold as the dew which was freezing on the grass, his fingers crooked in the mud, the arch of his back slumped to one side like a bridge washed over in the floods. He'd bust his own neck, that much was plain to see, the way that knob of bone stuck up like a bunched knuckle from his back. His face hung horizontal and Henry could make out the dip of dark where his tongue had fallen out of his mouth and Henry knew that he wasn't going to look at that face for anything, not for all the best rams on earth, not for a tup the size of a bath-tub, not for the salvation of his own soul.

Straight he went to the cow-shed, took an old blanket out of the box. He slipped the pin from its holes, taking care not to touch Gumbert's hair. He'd already started imagining that back shuddering behind him as he'd walked across the yard; he'd averted his eyes but still saw those hands unclaw and pull the pin from its knots, lift the yoke from his night-sodden shoulders, open the eyes in his corpse-yellow skin. Henry threw the blanket fast over Gumbert then tied him round with a rope, pulled him across the paddock and heaved him onto the milk-cart. He'd hated sitting up on that cart knowing what was behind him, feeling the ghosts crawling over him, thinking he might never be warm again. He'd gone out to the crossroads, taken the road to the south, tipped the last of Gumbert Frye, neighbour and thief, into one of the mist-moored bogs. His fingers shook as he got back up on the trap and clattered his way home. He'd got through a month's supply of smokes and brandy in that one night, but couldn't get to sleep for two days. He'd not noticed that old dog sniffing at the yoke abandoned in the paddock, padding around the trap, making his slow stiff way up the lane and turning left at the crossroads where the gallows used to stand and where Henry would have hung if anyone had found out about Gumbert Frye – never mind that he'd been trying to steal Henry's new tup, which was about the worst thing a man could do.

Except kill another one.

But no-one had found out what happened to Gumbert Frye.

They'd asked questions, they talked about it night after night, month after month until it was decided he'd wandered off drunk and got lost on the moor. You could do it sober and you could do it better drunk. And that was where everyone thought he was and where he'd been, and where until now he'd stayed hidden.

Henry Dibblewitch twitched back into life and picked up his peat spade. He thought about that night and all those years of guilt, of the constant companion of ghosts shivering below his skin, the way his heart still jumped and jigged when a shadow fell upon his back, or when the sun slipped behind a cloud and cast the gloom at his feet. He calculated the cost of not finding a wife who would put up with the way he screamed sometimes in the night. The loss he had made when he'd sold on the ram after just that one season. He stared at the brown clod still lying at his feet, then he thwacked that old Gumbert head until it disintegrated into the bits of bog which had kept it whole. He stamped his boots hard on the remains. He dug his way into that bank and got the rest of the Frye-thief out and bone by bone he obliterated that man from the earth. He'd had a face like the lakeland sky, people always said that about Gumbert, and at last, for Henry Dibblewitch, the rains had cleared and the blue horizons called the larks up from the heather.

Gumbert was no more, and like the gallows which had rotted and fallen and never been replaced, the old ghosts at the crossroads at last had gone. Henry tidied the peat-riddle, put the spade to his shoulder and went home.

Away on the moor an old dog howled as night came slow from the hills, rolled across the land like raven-wings, leached out the last of the light. Lonely and lonely those howls went on, but nobody heard, and they were lost in the rising wind and the rain that can curse or clear a midnight sky in a moment, maybe wash away one man's life, maybe give someone else back his own. Forty-two years that dog's been howling, howling in the dark lea of the hills. Maybe tonight, at last, he can lay down his old bones and sleep.

I Should Have Listened Harder...

It's night at Nertchinsk, and here we sleep three-deep to keep ourselves warm. Yesterday, the little man who made a fiddle out of nails and string didn't wake up with the rest of us. We should have known better than to put him at the bottom, but there it was. You have to take your turn. His face was flax-flower blue, his skin like wet putty, carrying the impress of his clothes and boots and our fingerprints as we stripped him down. We threw him into Disused Mineshaft number 15B, saw his pale form twist and fall, disappear into dark. No use digging ground for graves when it's four foot deep with frost; no use wasting half-decent clothes and boots. We let him take his fiddle with him. No-one else could get a tune out of it, anyway. It wasn't the worst thing I have ever done and I have done many things, and there are better places I have been than the lead mines of Nertchinsk.

The best thing I ever did was meet my Tzrika. The worst thing I ever did was lose him. I called him my son, but he wasn't. I found him in a place near Vitim where they said we could build ourselves a village, plant crops, make a new life. I'd been through the world and not liked it; I'd come back to Tomsk, soaked myself in good Russian vodka till my liver began to rot without waiting for the rest of me, without waiting for the coffin lid to close. I'd signed up for the New Frontier, got my pass and plot-number, bought my spade and sack of seeds and set off for the Promised Land. I met some other stragglers on the road, and when we finally made it through Vitim and reached the place we'd marked with a cross on our maps, we stopped. We unpacked our baggage, began to set up our tents, marked out our plots with sticks and string. And then the soldiers came up from the town behind us, told us the Grand Scheme was scrapped, though they couldn't tell us why. We could join the Jews at Birobidzhan, the New Israel a thousand miles to the east, or we could go down to Baikal and scrape a living from its shores. There are the roads, they said, and there are choices: you can go this way or that, and we'll be back in the morning.

But we'd come too far and could go no further, so we stood by our collapsing shelters, gripping our tent poles sharpened into stakes and refused to go.

'Leave!' they told us, and we stood by our pathetic village and shouted back our *Nos*. They levelled their guns and shot us down, told us one way or the other we would be gone. And we were. There was me and the boy and two old women who were left to tramp the track to Baikal. We got there – or rather me and Tzrika did. One of the women got sick on the way and the other stayed to look after her.

'Go,' she said. 'We'll catch you up.' But we all knew she wouldn't, and she didn't. And so me and the boy arrived at Baikal, and it was early summer and warm. I found work on the boats and a place to live, and Tzrika stayed home twisting ropes into nets, and against all the odds we were happy. We dawdled along the Baikal's banks, me and Tzrika, when I wasn't working. We got our month of fish, some blubber-oil for our lamps; we smoked fish-skin into leather, traded it for flour and tea, and sold Tzrika's nets back to the boats. We took walks, made bows and arrows out of wych-elm, skewered rabbits and marmot for the pot. We told each other stories as we mended our trousers, darned our socks, drank a bit of vodka with our tea. We visited the Caves of the Lonely Sea where the waves will tell a man his future as they lap against the walls on a Midsummer's Eve.

But we were late.

It was autumn.

And we didn't know the Baikal at all.

They call it a sea, the Baikal, and it's like a sea but it isn't. Fifty miles wide from shore to shore and three hundred miles long it stretches: it is London to Paris, Kiev to Odessa; it is the entire width of Iceland. These are all places I have been, but nowhere was as beautiful and blue as the Baikal, with its basalt cliffs running sheer into the water and down to the centre of the earth. It is a windswept width of water – everyone will tell you so. It has from the north the *Gara* wind which lifts the surface six dark yards into the air, sends the water crashing back again, makes toothpicks out of fishing boats and trees, flings fish overland for a mile. From the south-west comes the *Koultouk*, milder, wetter, slapping the surface into wet curls, painting it with streaks of white, sending the scree slipping from the hills down to muddy its banks; in between comes the *Bargouzine*, chasing from east to west like a djinn, hard and cruel, quick and vicious, bringing ice and sleet and hail which cut like cat-whips soaked in frozen milk. And then, when the sun is low and the days are short, when it freezes in its long winter, we think the Baikal sleeps and forgets. We dance with our skates upon its skin, run dog-sleds up and down its back. It is deep, so deep: a thousand fathoms sink beneath our feet as we glide like mites across the surface of its eye. We trade from it, we steal from it, tea merchants from China pass as if it is their Right of Way. But the Baikal knows, and of a sudden it cracks and yawns a gap of fifteen miles, and whoever is there on the ice at that moment is lost without mercy and gone.

And just when the Baikal was beginning to slumber, when the mercury was already sluggish in the glass, I got the boils down my back like a spill of summer rain. I covered them with creosote, rubbed them with oil, strapped on a babushka of butter and gunpowder, but nothing worked. I'm a foreigner here; I ask advice, I take it. I butchered a Baikal seal down its middle and wore it warm as a cape. The boatman was shouting, 'Last boat out before it's winter!' but the boils were not cured and the skipper demanded Tzrika in my place.

'No boy for the boat, no work for you next season,' said the skipper, hard as those Baikal basalt cliffs. 'We're not taking some boil-infested bastard to infect the rest of the crew. It happens,' he said and shrugged his shoulders, 'I can't go out with one man down.'

What could I do? What could *we* do? Tzrika was eager; *I will be a man*, he said, and the skipper agreed. I think about that now, what I should have said and done, but it's always too late. I never knew that fiddle-player's name, but he used to say that no man gets to pick his own tune, and he was right.

I stayed on the shore of the Baikal wrapped in my sealskin, and the boat went out and with it went my Tzrika. Two days I waited, while the Gara wind growled down early from the mountains like a hungry bear woken too soon from its sleep. Back came the boat in bits, and gone were the catch, half the boat-house, all the nets. And then came that skipper, hard-ridged and red from the wind, death written right across his face, tramping resolute across the shingle. I didn't wait for him to tell me what he had done. I shook that sealskin from off my shoulders and smothered him with it there on those ice-encrusted stones, the clot-rotten seal-blood black upon his face, his gaping mouth the new-dug grave by which I had been waiting. Waiting for the only son I ever had, or ever would have, and my Tzrika, blown from off the bridge of that skipper's boat like a leaf and swallowed in the blackness of the Baikal.

Should I forgive the skipper? Should he forgive me? I don't know. What I do know is it's a long way from Baikal to Nertchinsk: four hundred miles of hard country over the Yat and the Yablonoyy mountains. Take my advice and plan your murder well into the winter, then at least you'll stay at Ullan Ude till the spring. Not so for me. I took those mountains with my hands in fetters just as the winds began to call and the snow was trailing in. I wore my jerkin of sealskin, burned a map into the inside to plan for my escape. But Nertchinsk isn't like Sakhalin, where people throw themselves into the sea and always drown. Keeps the prison populations down, they say, which is good in a place where there are always more, like rats, to take their place. I used to dream of being sent to Sakhalin, setting off into that sea like so many have done before. I would cling to a raft of driftwood the fifty miles to Japan. That's all it is: two peoples, two continents and only fifty miles apart. Who thinks of that? Only those of us who do nothing but work and sleep, work and sleep, which is what we do at Nertchinsk. We sleep, we work, and sometimes we think. It isn't allowed, but we do it anyway. I think of my Tzrika and know I will never have another son. Not now. Not ever. Not after Nertchinsk. They tell me it's the lead.

I Should Have Listened Harder...

We dig the mines the old way, with pickaxes; we smelt the ore the cheap way, on a turnbole, a huge wooden platform raised above the fire. It is mounted on gimbals so we can swing it to the prevailing wind to fire up the flames. It keeps some of us from freezing; makes sure we can work another day. We sit in our heaps next to the turnbole, wrapped in our blankets, no longer caring of the fleas and lice that survive the cold of the night. We tell each others stories about how things might have been. I lie there in my sealskin jacket and listen to the wolves. They remind me of the echoes in the Caves of the Lonely Sea. And I think: I think I should have gone there earlier. I should have planted my ear to those cold cave-walls the whole midsummer-night through, and then maybe, maybe, we would still be mending nets together and darning socks and drinking tea warmed with vodka and wallowing with seals in the brief summer of the Baikal when the elks come down from the hills and the water is warm.

These are the things which I have done and the places I have been.

It is my turn on the bottom and I have taken off my sealskin jacket. Use it if you find it, for I will not. I see it lying at the edge of fire-light, half in darkness. I turn my head away. I burrow below the shivering bodies of my workmates.

'Pile on, lads,' I murmur. 'Pile yourselves high and bury me deep.'

It is dark. Strangely, it is quite warm. I cannot move. I will never move again, except to Disused Mineshaft 15B. My very own cave in my lonely, sonless sea.

We work, we sleep, sometimes we think, and as I lie here I think maybe there is another summer somewhere; maybe Tzrika is already there and if I listen hard enough maybe I will hear him and better still, maybe, if I keep still enough, he will hear me.

We work, we sleep.

And then there comes the time when we no longer have to think, and this is mine.

Maze

It was the Colonel put the plan into my head. We'd been sitting in the sun when the boys came by and punched me into standing. *Tom-o-Hoop* they called it, throwing sticks and stones – points for hitting arms and legs, elbows and head. When they'd gone, I collapsed in a bruise and began to cry. That was when the Colonel told me to pull myself together and stop being a ninny.

'Go and wash your face, boy, and stop that snivelling at once! Do you think I'd let any one of my soldiers make such a weeping-willow of himself? Certainly not! You mustn't let the enemy grind you down. Look at me and the dear wife: weren't we smashed to smithereens without so much as a by-your-leave? Don't you think it hurt to have our ribs splintered and the blood squirted from our skin? Do you think we enjoyed being buried alive under what was once our home? It's dangerous times, and in the face of danger, my boy, what we need is a plan.'

Plenty we planned that night and I never even went home, and when we'd done I lay down under my maze and went to sleep.

Mother cried and walked all night through the village shouting my name, and at dawn she went to the Justice.

'My lad's missing and his bloody shirt is snagged on the wall by Drustan's!' Mam yelled, and pulled the Justice out till everyone knew that the washerwoman's son was missing. And everyone knew about Peder and Drustan, Mark and John Davey and all the nasty little doings they did, so the Justice rounded the lot of them up. John Davey and Mark started blubbing and blaming the other two, and Peder and Drustan stayed stumm. Then down went the whole village to the tow-path and followed the blood to the weir, saw the crushed grass, the shoe-scuffs, found Peder's hat sticking up accusingly in the silt.

37

'Three days!' the Justice bellows. 'Bang them up in the stocks and see if they talk!'

People gathered round them, threw cabbage stalks, whispered about murder and the gallows, then back home they went and laughed and said, 'We'll give those bully-boys another day before we let them home to their beds!'

But the boys didn't know and thought they were going to hang, so when the press-gang sergeant appeared at midnight and whispered release, they signed up in an instant whilst he unpicked the stock-locks, and away they went to help old Wellington defend the Peninsula's southern shores.

They'd always been like that, those boys, picking on people quieter than themselves.

'Maisie walks the maze,' they'd say, even though my name was Tom. They'd pelt me with rotten apples, tip me upside down, make my lunch-piece fall out into the mud.

I never said a word. Mostly because I didn't have a tongue.

Mam'd scrub me off, tell me they was worse than cattle-poop and twice as thick, and I'd watch the tear-track trickle down her face. Mam and Tommy would have their bits of bread and jam then she'd get back to her washing and out I'd go again and walk the maze.

It's a grand place, though the house is just a pile of rubble since the mine collapsed and took half the hillside with it. On a night, you can hear the Colonel and his wife still playing their piano underneath the stones, and when the wind blows hard, it sifts out bits of books about the Sunny Plains of India where trees grow upside down and all the animals live forever. I found a box once, with snuff in it still dry. Mam was well pleased when I took it home, and saved it up for Sundays.

The maze is cool and damp and quiet and dark. You've to crawl through the overgrown branches, round the corners and curves, running your fingers through the leaves, along the switch-back hedges. The other boys shout outside and throw stones over the hedge-tops but they won't come in. They followed me once but got lost and scared and John Davey even

started to cry. Peder and Drustan got to the middle but when
they looked for me I was gone. They took ages getting out
and frightened each other half to death with stories of how
the Colonel had boiled me up in his pot and how I'd never
cried out 'cos I'd got no tongue and even if I'd had one, that
old Colonel would have sliced it out of my head with his knife
and fried it to a sizzle on his fire. They never knew there was
a tunnel running underground, starting by the sundial behind
the bramble-scrub and lilac, and going the way down to the
river. It was the Colonel showed me, told me stories of the
smugglers who brought the stolen tea and tobacco in from the
barges, sold it to the men at the mines. That was how the Big
House got built in the first place, he said, from all that money
pinched from the taxman. Maybe that was why it collapsed. He
told me lots of tales, did the Colonel, and he and his wife kept
company with me, playing games or paddling in the stream.
They liked the way I wailed and harried the tow-path walkers,
made them jump and quicken their pace. I was proud of my
wail; it was the only sound I could make.

The plan had worked, and after two days in the maze I tip-toed
home and Mam got such a shock she dropped the chicken she'd
been strangling and it ran round the yard dragging its head
between its feet. She laughed and sneezed the last of the snuff
up when I finally got over how the Colonel and me had killed
a rabbit and caught the blood and laid it out by the path; how
I'd crept about that night and stolen Peder's cap and snaggled
my shirt on Drustan's wall. I never actually mentioned the
Colonel – I knew that Mam didn't hold with such things – but
I knew I couldn't have done it without him.

'You tricked 'em proper,' chuckled Mam, all proud, and then
she shined up my bruises, spat on my hair and off we went to
the Justice.

'Two days he's been lying in the fallow-field unconscious,'
says Mam to all his questions. 'Couldn't move or shout or cry
for help! That's what those boys have done and don't we all
know it?'

The villagers gathered and nodded their heads and the

Justice said 'Hmmm,' and gave me a penny, told me not to spend it all at once. And then we saw that the stocks were deserted, their empty sockets casting hollow patterns in the sun, and we all stood around and looked at each other, but no-one knew what had happened or where they had gone.

Drustan and Mark and John Davey went to Spain with old Wellington, and Drustan, Mark and John Davey never came back. Peder, the tailor's boy, dragged into the village eighteen months later. Winter, all cold and raggled, his backpack hanging by a broken strap.

'Poor Peder,' whispered everybody behind his back, for back he'd come, but he'd come without his hands: blown off by a musket when he was sitting by a campfire making his tea.

Peder comes into the maze, pushing his way through the hedges, bit by bit, stumbling here and there. Eventually he gets to the middle and sits on the sundial and cries. I hear him from my underground cave, sobbing slowly, quietly. It's a week past since he's been back and though I've heard him try before, this is the first time he's reached the middle. It's starting to rain, quite soft at first then harder and harder, thumping hailstones on the ground and bouncing off the stones. I creep up the steps and pop out my head. There he is. Just sitting, hailstones gathering in his collar. I crawl out and stand in front of him and he is so surprised he slips off the sundial and crashes to the ground. He's got no hands to stop him so his stumps hit first and he howls in pain as the skin-scars stretch and start to tear. He just lies there on his face, whimpering.

Then someone's standing tall behind me, tapping me on the shoulder.

'Go on, you witless nincompoop!' says the Colonel into my ear. 'You don't think I'd leave one of my own alone on the battlefield getting pounded by enemy fire?'

So I help Peder up, take his elbows, drag him along on his knees and into the tunnel, down the steps, one by one. I sit him beside me; show him my game of *Tom-o-Hoop* which I've made from some willow withies and a big oak stick I've jammed into the wall. He looks dazed, cradles one stump inside the other, rocking gently, so I light a candle and rest it on the rock beside him. He's looking around and around about him, first at me, then at the stairs, then at me again, then at the tunnel leading off into the gloom. His face is going all crumply and his head is nodding from side to side and side to side, faster and faster, then all of a sudden his voice cracks and he starts to laugh and laugh and laugh, great globes of tears falling to the dust about his fraying boots.

He comes down quite often, does Peder, and now and then we play games or paddle in the underground stream or maybe play blindfold Buffet and Bung. Sometimes we wail at the people walking by the river bank or scare the boys by throwing things up and out over the maze. The Colonel and his wife have moved back to India. They asked me to go with them, but Peder said, 'Don't go, Tom. Let's you and me stay here forever.'
    And one day, after Peder'd dragged some old gunpowder sacks down from the mine, stay there forever we did.

The old stocks are gone, and the Justice and the Washerwoman and the Tailor-man are long time dead. Nothing stays the same except the place where the mine took away half the hill. There's another boy climbs there over the stones of the Big House, listens for the Colonel's piano playing in the wind. He crawls through the dark and damp of the maze on his belly, feels his way through its rabbit-warren ways. He sits against the stump of the sundial which no longer tells the time. He doesn't mind. He leans his head back into the lilac, listens for the noise of the river which echoes up through the collapsed tunnel, tinkers amongst its blown-up stones. He found a small withy-hoop one time, and a piece of candle. When it's really quiet and the leaves have stilled on their branches and the air is suspended between evening and dark and all the bees have burrowed into the ground to sleep, he thinks he hears voices, thinks he hears the sound of boys playing, of feet splashing in water, a faint wailing coming up from the stones. I've hands, says one, I've a tongue, says the other, and he hears them rustling and running through the maze.

'All the way to India,' thinks the boy for no reason he knows, and stands up to follow. He twists the withy-hoop into his pocket, turns his back to the dial; he doesn't feel quite so lonely now and decides that perhaps it's time to head for home, maybe give his Mam that old snuff-box he found yesterday, just sitting in full view on a rock by the river as the water scratched it's back down the weir, and the willows shook in the warmth of an early evening wind.

Message from Asinara

There is a boat far out on the Tyrrhenian Sea, prow-bent for Sardinia. A man on the deck furrows his brow, strains for the white of sand, the shadow of hills. He has been a week travelling: by punt, paddle-steamer, horse and carriage; the last few yards on foot. He flung his baggage into the first boat to take him across the sea. The skipper took the money and directions, asked no questions, pulled at his cap, told his boys to cast off.

Elbows on the rickety rails, the man gazes over the violet sunset water and breathes tar and fish-scales, smells the hot rum he holds in his hands. At the end of the deck two crewmen sit smoking, their backs bare and black, salted from sea and sweat, hard hands paying out the rope, slowly setting the net. They scratch at their bristles, stare at the dolphins blowing in the wake, steal glances at the stranger leaning against the rails.

'What's his story?' says Silvano, letting go a bit more line.

'Who cares, long as he's paying,' answers Pedestro.

'Hope he's already stumped up; he'll go in if he's not careful. Those rails weren't meant for brooding on.'

'Best watch he don't,' grumbles old man Pedestro. 'Bad for the fishing is that. Poisons the water, does a drowning.'

Silvano knocks out his pipe; relights it. The old ash glows red by his feet. It catches the stranger's eye and he looks startled; moves away further down the deck into darkness.

'Can't even see him now, blast it,' mutters Pedestro. 'First we'd know'd be the splash and crush of him under the keel, then no doubt he'll get himself stuck in the net and make a wreck of that too. Bloody bastard.'

Silvano laughs, feels his arm tugged against the weight of the net. 'Hold off grumbling – we've hit a shoal. Either that or your man's in the water already! Get off your arse and pull!'

The boat heaves to one side as the men haul the ropes round the winch heads and begin to reel in the net. Silvano's pipe is shoved into his breeks, the unused tobacco smouldering warm against his leg. The stranger moves out of the darkness, comes forward to watch the show, refills his rum-cup from a flask. He sees a skin of silver erupt, a thousand fishbacks breaking the water, dancing under the prow-lamps, fins gilded, flashing, an army of tiny Turks drawing scimitar and sword. Silvano and Pedestro lend hard muscles to the winch levers, backwards, forwards, backwards, forwards, rasping out a song between clenched teeth to keep them in rhythm:

> *Winch 'em, rope 'em, rig 'em, reel 'em,*
> *Land 'em, crate 'em, scrape 'em, peel 'em,*
> *Gut 'em, cut 'em, salt 'em, sell 'em,*
> *Beat 'em, eat 'em, send 'em to hell 'em.*

The stranger edges forward, hugs the darkness below the sail, doesn't want to interfere, feels his foot tapping out the tune; hears the boil of fin and tail being hauled yard by yard through the surface of the sea, alongside the boat, up the rough wooden battens of the side. The winches scream as the load comes over the bulwarks; Silvano and Pedestro jam the levers, quickly throw open the trap-door to the hold. A hundred thousand fish staring, leaping, gaping, flipping, finally tires the net. They are disgorged across the deck, noise shimmering like leaves in a forest, splinters of ice skimming across a frozen lake. The stranger barely has time to open his mouth before he is tugged from his feet. Then Silvano and Pedestro are lunging their long fish-brooms across the surface, a thin yard of bristles sweeping the escaping shoal down the boards and into the hole. Long practice ensures they leap light amongst mercurial swirls, catching every deserter trying to slipper its way back to the sea. When they are done they throw the brooms to the scaled deck, slam shut the hatch. Sit back on their capstans, retrieve their pipes and begin to smoke.

Down in the hole the stranger splutters, screams in silence; sardines in his hair, his boots, his cuffs, his shirt, his mouth, his pockets, his skin. It is ten minutes before he is heard and

a rope is dropped. Ten more minutes as his fingers slip and
slide from the hemp. Five more before he lies beached up on
the deck, green-lit and ghostly, shining, shimmering, shivering
at the stars.

I think I am crying, a dreadful thing in front of these hard
men but I don't care. I gasp the air and taste fish. My nostrils
open and close but there is a horrid stickiness about them of
gut and glair. I dare not open my eyes. I feel as if I'm in the
belly of a whale. Without warning a barrel of salt water is
thrown upon me, the shock of cold forcing me to my knees,
arms waving wildly, my shouts mad as a shot boar. Another
barrel knocks me back down but the sailors have me by the
armpits and drag me away, roll me in a blanket, lay me on a
bed of old crates. I croak out thanks and find my throat filled
with deep dark rum, my ears ringing with laughter. Something
presses uncomfortably into my back – something in the pocket
of my coat which has somehow wrung itself around me in the
struggle to survive a smothering of sardines. The realisation
of what it is that is causing my discomfort makes me splutter
and the sailors, fearing I am choking, force more liquor down
my throat as if this will somehow help. My throat contracts
with sobs, my gut wrenches as I spit my anger and my thin joy
out into the world. With shaking fingers I extract the object
from my coat. It is the only thing I possess, apart from the
clothes on my back and a few pennies in the bank. I rub my
thumb over its impress and feel its warmth, its life, begin to
seep within me. We're kin, it and I: fish offal, spat back from
the shores of death.

From the awful rubble I picked up that button. The silver
was scorched black, but the wings of a Prussian eagle shone
out in gold. It was all that was left of my paper-museum,
being the only thing not made of paper. My whole house was
gone too, the glass blown from the windows, the roof-trusses
hanging like hairs from what was left of the frame. It might
have been a carcass dug from a peat-bog for all that was left
of it. The outline was there, but the substance had gone. How
that fire started I don't know. Maybe I left a lamp burning

when I went to lie in my bed. I had been studying my papers late into the night, adding to my lists, categorising the latest arrivals, making inventory and index. I collected old maps, botanical watercolours, zoological plates, documents of all and any kind. I had a marriage licence from fourteenth century Florence which bore the name of a minor Medici; I had a copy of the Icelandic government's minutes sprawled across a side of seal; I had a book covered in elephant vellum which told of the slaughter of some Indian tribe. And now all I had was that button.

It had arrived three years ago in a letter from an old friend:

'*My dear Orlando,*

As you know, I am in Sardinia studying the albino donkeys of Asinara. Yesterday I dined at a rather inferior inn located on the aptly named Desolation Point. I ordered hare – you'll remember it is a favourite of mine, but not when it is as tough as leather and smells of armpits. I sent it back in under thirty seconds! I was given instead the only other thing on the menu, a tunny-fish pie. It was good, if a little fat, and when I commented on this to the waiter – a smiling fellow despite all the customers' complaints of which there were not a few – he professed no surprise, but dug his hand into his apron and took out a button. Placing it on the grubby tablecloth he said he found it whilst doing the gutting that morning. He was then summoned away, but I handed him a handsome tip and pocketed the button. That evening I took a sup at the bar and learnt a quite horrifying tale apropos the button and the fish, which thank God I never heard whilst I was eating. The story was this: there is an island hereabouts used as a prison. During the last wars, the Italians closeted their captives in the place in the most appalling conditions. Many died of diphtheria, cholera and the like, notwithstanding their war-wounds. So many were the fatalities – sometimes hundreds in one day – that

*the corpses were packed onto barges, taken out into the
bay and sunk. After such a tale, which I have no doubt
is true, I cannot say I feel inclined to keep the trophy
of what practically amounts to my having partaken in
cannibalism!*

*So here it is, old friend. It is yours. I know you
collect such curios and I am glad to see the back of it.
The only thing I ask is that you hide it away before I
visit, as I fear my stomach could not take it. Incidentally,
I have found out that not only buttons have been found
in these fish. Teeth and rings are not uncommon, though
generally the bodies are stripped of valuables before
being fed to the fish. Once, I gather, a rather fine gold
locket was found still bearing the portraits of a man
and woman. It is surmised the man swallowed the thing
in order to keep it close to his heart and out of the
pocket of his gaolers. And yet it ended up on the slab
of a Sardinian fishmonger. Some things in life are so
sad one has to laugh in order not to weep.*

*From your good friend,
Jeremiah Hoogenstraater.'*

When I had scrambled my way from my bed, having been
woken by the splintering of cabinet cases and the collapse
of shelves, I stood silently on the grass of the paddock and
watched my life burn to nothing. Though the river was close
by, there was no-one to pass a line of buckets and the pump was
long since broken, the pipe perished and cracked. My closest
neighbours were two miles across the downs: the very reason
I had picked this place, small as it was, in which to pursue the
joys of my life. While I stood, the tears running down my face, a
line of cupboards collapsed one upon the other and spilled their
contents into the flames. It felt as if my ribs were splintering
in the cave of my chest, so deep were my sobs.

Hours later I wandered through the wreckage, kicking at
the ash. I found a pair of boots and some clothes in a chest
which had withheld its contents from the worst. They didn't fit

well, having been my father's: a man of considerably more bulk than me. As I kicked through the inches of ash I hit something hard and saw it twinkle amongst the grey matting. I bent stiffly, like an automaton, and picked it up. I feel it now: the button is still warm from the ashes and cinder, like the roots pawed up by deer after a gorse-fire. The smell is charcoal and acrid, smouldering beneath a drizzle of dawn mist. An unbearable sadness settles upon me as I stand and watch the fine stained-glass panes from the window still melting into the stinking mud. Of my library all that is left are a few twisted brackets, a scorched bolt skew-whiff in the pocked wall. Of the quartos and folios there is nothing. Twenty years of notebooks are black and ash. The roof-beams creak above me; a tarry soot covers everything, settling in my hair, upon my skin. It is too drear to stand in the wreck of a room where everything once valued is destroyed. So I put the button in my pocket, turned my back and left.

On my boat in the Bay of Esmeralda, stinking and filled with rum, I think of men who eat fish and fish who eat men and men who feed other men to the fish. A pale spike of light yawns across the sky and I thank God for another day. I breathe the dawn, the button warm in my hand. A sudden impulse seizes me and I fling the button which led me here in an arc across the waters. I smile, put the bottle to my mouth; do not watch as the button sinks below the waves.

'Let it go,' I laugh to myself, intoxicated, clear though the moment is as a shaft of sunlight in a cellar. 'Life is to fall and survive, and the adventure is in not knowing where you will land. We've another day to live, you and I, brother. Maybe one day we'll meet again.'

Immediately after that I vomit hard and loud; lie wretched, sobbing upon the salty boards, all thoughts long seeped from my head.

Four hours later we land.

Eleven years on and I am still at Desolation Point and have amassed a small curio museum; the tourists pay an entrance fee which keeps me going and Jeremiah has given me the loan of a small cottage on his property. Silvano sometimes calls and we drink deep of the island's dark rum. He misses Pedestro, who died several years ago, tangled in the nets, hauled overboard and drowned beneath the keel. I visit the fishmongers often. I have several buttons in my collection and, indeed, a rather fine locket. But I will eat nothing bigger than a sardine and sometimes even they make me feel a trifle sick.

Men that eat fish. Fish that eat men. There are things in life it takes a lifetime to understand and I feel I am just beginning. Or perhaps, as so often these days, it is only the rum.

The Boot-Tree Man

Sunday morning, before the church bell has rung for mass and I'm busy scraping out the gibbet cages. Only three more to do and the old pickled heads to knock off the poles down by the bridge. You'd think I'd hate this work – the smells and the excrement, ribbons of green, decomposing flesh getting caught in my buttons and cuffs – but I don't. It's a job puts you in mind of being someone special. Folk'll cross the street to avoid touching you and I've a special tankard at the tavern. I can't swim in the river nor shake nobody by the hand, and I've a particular pew in back of the church, up the balcony by the pigeon roost. Gives me the chance to snooze off during the sermon. I like it, this being someone apart, someone special. The only drawback, says uncle, is the girls.

'Hard to meet 'em, hard to keep 'em. Best keeping it in the family.'

He's lining me up for his daughter who's got the look of being milk-fed all her life, her skin white as veal, and a frizz of ginger hair. I like the way it curls on her neck and becomes an orange aureole in the sun, but she hates it and always strangles it up in some bonnet or bow or smothers it flat under a scarf. It might be mine some day, I think, but I'm young yet and time to find something better.

Pigeon Wynd, crooked and narrow. Night-lights flicker in glass cases, wind licking the candles, playing dip-and-twist with the flames. Shop signs creak on rusty poles and the barber's red-n-white spins in glee. Half-way up the street, a window taps in its frame. The baker thinks he hears a dog whining; feels sorry for it out in the snow. He listens to the night, watches the stars, then rolls himself out of bed. The frost on the windows is beginning to melt and it's not so cold now the stoking-boy has fired the ovens in the cellars below. The Watchman is at the door, his staff raised slightly, his cloak well-wrapped, half-bottle warming in his pocket. The baker puts on his whites, opens the door and motions his brother in. They always spend the while together, one beginning his shift, one ending, sitting quietly at the big table having a sup, chatting vaguely about their days and nights. It is pretty much the last thing they're expecting when the dog from next door comes flying out of a window, a high-pitched howl as it hits the parlour roof and falls with a ghastly thud and crack onto the paving stones of the baker's backyard. They both of them leap to their feet and the stoking-boy scurries up from the cellar, hair full of debris dislodged from the ceiling as the dog hit. The baker gets to his back door and has momentary trouble opening it because he's forgotten to slip the bolt. He wrenches it hard and it slams back into the parlour, blown by a gust of wind which extinguishes the candle on the table. They stare at the dog, eyes rolled back in its head, blood seeping from its nose, yellow foam on its lolling tongue, and they haven't crossed the two paces to reach it when another form comes hurtling at them through the dark, and right above their heads two feet bounce and recoil, bounce and recoil, all the while kicking and convulsing, as the man in the noose above tears at his throat, the rope tightening all the while, his windpipe slowly crushed and closed, blood trickling from the corners of his eyes and through one perforated eardrum. Far up above in the silent black of heaven, a shooting star traces an arc across the sky and disappears, then another, and another as the Pleiades play out their games.

I am called in to cut down the body and take a look at the knot, uncle being away taking care of a big party getting swung in the next shire. There is no going through the front door for me with my profession, so it's round the back I step and into the alley behind Pigeon Wynd. It's a rather mean street called The Crook on account of having a couple of bends you could get round a hair-pin. The baker's house stands out, being the only one with a corpse dangling from its attic window, and though there aren't any flies, it being dead of winter, there are neighbours a-plenty, gathered and gawping, tongues wagging so loud you could hear them half-way down The Crook. They recognise the creak of my barrow and clear a path to the gate, and them that's got prime space in the yard have to give it up and go back for fear I'll catch them on my way past.

It's a tricky business getting him down, for it's most definitely a he – he's got no breeks on and the rigor is quite pronounced under his johns. His feet are bare and blue, but it's an odd thing that he's all dressed up on top and I see the twinkle of a gold fob struck across his waistcoat and a handkerchief all silk and tidy sticking from out a pocket. It strikes me funny they've not cut him down already, so I shouts for the Watchman and he comes to the door, a little red and slurred, reeking of the brandy he's taken to steady his nerves.

'Have you not been up the attic yet?' I asks, and points to where the rope is coming out of the gable window.

'It's not the baker's,' says he, 'even though it's up atop his house. The whole run of three belongs to the boot-tree man: this one here, the one next door and the one next door to that. We've tried the boot-tree man and there's no answer and the chandler says his attic's locked from the top and he couldn't get up if he wanted. We've sent word for the boot-tree man but no-one knows where he is.'

I glance up at the blue feet and wonder, but no-one seems to think it's him, this man dangling in the dawn. In fact, no-one seems to recognise him at all.

'I should break the door down, Mr Watchman, sir,' says I, but he scowls at me and says,

'No doubt you would in your neck of town, but round here we're respectable folk and don't go round breaking into people's houses when they're not at home.'

'Well, well,' says I, and starts leaning the ladder against the wall. 'A nice part of town you're in, but where I stay we don't throw men out of windows, leastwise not when they're still attached to a good piece of rope.'

'It's a strange sort of knot, is that.' I'm pointing to the man lying on the slab, gold fob still in his waistcoat, silk folded neat at his pocket. The doctor's fine me being here; we're colleagues really, with me bringing him corpses to dissect, and him giving me the leftovers to bury when he's done. We both lean closer and squint at it – the rope's a good rope made of fine cord, treble twisted, probably new as there's a dust about it when it's touched and it has a fine smell of fresh jute.

'Not the chandler's then?' he asks, and pokes at it with a pair of forceps.

'Not likely,' I answers. 'We get ours there and he's nothing so good.'

'Who would use rope like this?' he asks, and sets us thinking of who uses any rope at all. The men on the canal boats, anyone who's packing and crating to do, the pulley-operators down at the warehouse, the slaughter-house for halting and hanging, the tunny-men for cooping their barrels... and then all of a sudden I know where I've seen that exact same golden dust, smelt that smell. It was in church last Sunday. Like I say, I'm up top by the pigeon nests, and right behind me is the stairwell that goes down to the ground and up to the bell tower, and just below the tower there's an open hatchway so you can lean through and touch the bells, set them going by hand. Its been that way a long time since, from when the church doubled as a look-out tower, and if you saw the enemy running up the hill and over the city walls you didn't waste time getting down the stairs to the bell-ropes, you just leaned through the hatchway and set them going by hand. 'Course now, in modern times, there wasn't much need of it so it had rather been left to rot and from where I sat, legs stretched out on the pew in front of me, lulled by doo-coos, my eyes would drift here and there, and often as not end up at the open hatchway, seeing the ropes sway in the breeze, wondering what it would be like to lean right in and tipple over, watching the pigeons perch and poop over the edge. I tell the doctor I've thought of something, and tell him where I'm off, and straightaway I sets off down Gargle Lane and through Dark Street and Lime Road until I reach the minister's cottage and the church. I go right in the back entrance like I always do and up the stairs, across the gallery. I lean through the hatchment and count the ropes: one, two, three, four – and there it is. Number five. Cut clean through with a knife. I go and bang on the minister's door, forgetting it's barely dawn, and he leans out like he always does and asks who's dead.

'Who's dead?' he'll go. 'Somebody better bloody well be, to get me up so early.'

'We've a definite corpse, cold as yesterday's mutton,' I reassure him, 'and doctor says you've to come and see if you know him. No-one else does.'

He pulls his head in from the cold, grumbling, and slams the window shut. He's up and ready in a few minutes, blowing on his hands, hawking and spitting out last night's tobacco. He keeps apace with me, and close. It's uncomfortable and I'm not used to it, but it's his way of being kind, saying I'm no different to any other sinner. While we walk back up Lime Road I tell him the story of what's occurred. He says nothing, just nods his head as if a man got tumbled out of a window every week. We're quiet again till we reach the junction of Dark Street and Gargle, and then I ask him about the rope.

'When did you get the new bell ropes in, vicar?'

'Er, bell ropes ... let's see. Last Saturday. Found them working on it when I came back from exorcising Mrs Clodburn's husband again. Ghosts indeed. Does she think we're still in the Dark Ages?'

'So,' says the doctor, handing the vicar and me some tea with a good slug of rum in it to clear the corpse-stink from our mouths. 'If the ropes only went up Saturday and you saw them Sunday, and today's Thursday, that means they were cut some time between Monday and Wednesday. Didn't the bell ringers notice anything? Like there were only four ropes and not five and one of them had nothing in his hands?'

'We've only got the full set on Sundays, and Thursday night when they practice,' mumbles the vicar into his tea, 'old Ted comes in to ring for the morning and evening service, and he's practically blind. I've got a queue of youngsters wanting to take the job on but Ted says he's been doing it for sixty-nine years and he'll do it another sixty-nine if God grants him.'

'If he goes on that long I'll not be here to cut him up and find out why. I'd best get some tips from Mrs Clodburn's husband, come back and haunt my successor, whisper suggestions in his ear.'

The doctor always did like a laugh, especially when he's finished a long job like this, and the body's finally wrapped in burlap, only the toes sticking out, and he can relax with his rum and tea and stuffing his pipe.

'It's a pity we don't know who he is. Thought you might know, vicar. A new face in church, or maybe an old one, or someone you've run into on parish business. He had some rather fine dental work – proper ivory, not dead men's teeth. Hand-carved and fitted. And I'm guessing he was used to wearing several heavy rings on one hand – there's various indentations on the fingers. Surprising the murderer didn't take the fob as well. Why take the rings and leave a valuable watch and fob?'

A look of horror spreads over the vicar's face and his cup rattles violently against the saucer as he sets it down on the table. His eyes widen as an idea takes hold and spreads. He shakes his head to clear it but it is there to stay.

'What if the murderer didn't take the rings? What if the man took them off before he came out because he didn't want them seen?'

He looks up at the doctor and his face take on a tinge of green, as if he's about to boke.

'I think it might be Bishop Bartleby. It's hard to tell. I mean, he's not in his habit and he's a bit, well, a bit out of shape.'

He's right there – a hanged man's not a pretty sight. The face is all distended as the blood gets pumped up and can't get back down again. Purple is usual but black is not uncommon, like our friend next door on his back. The eyes get all bloodshot and sticky-out and the tongue is usually a good six inches longer than you'd expect and thicker than a blood sausage.

The vicar is rubbing his forehead with the sweaty palm of his hand. 'We'd need to check, but dear Lord Jesus! He was always boasting about his teeth. How when he'd visited the Eternal City he'd had them specially made by a Syrian, using only the finest ivory. He'd got a big sculpture of some squatting religious – a Buddha, I think – which he'd got from some backward

Indian country. He was very proud that he was chipping at it bit by bit to make the clerical teeth. Said he was converting the heathen statue into a Christian thing. The Bishop found it mighty amusing and told us time and time again. But what would he be doing in Pigeon Wynd? And why is he wearing those clothes?'

'And where are his shoes?' puts in the doctor.

'And his breeks?' says I.

We all go quiet and ruminate on our thoughts while the doctor pours out another tot. It's a mystery and no doubt about it. A dead bishop hanging out an attic in Pigeon Wynd in the middle of the night with a bell-rope round his neck and no breeks nor shoes. And of course, there was the dog.

About a month later, the snow melted of a sudden, and we'd a week of blue skies and a warm wind blowing south-south-west. The baker and the Watchman still met in the early hours and still worried over the case. Where had the boot-tree man gone? What was the bishop doing in his attic, for Bartleby it was, and who threw him out the casement? The church closed ranks – within two weeks a replacement bishop was up and running and nothing more was said. The Watchman only knew that Bartleby's rings had been found in his desk and his working clobber all accounted for. The mystery began to unravel when the Watchman took a stand one night and called me in. Along the Crook to Pigeon Wynd and not yet dawn, sledgehammer in my hand.

'Heave that door in and take a look,' says the Watchman in front of the boot-tree man's.

'It stinks like the devil,' grumbles the baker, 'and since it's been warm I can't smell nothing else.'

I give the Watchman a look, as if to say, 'Didn't I tell you to bash in that attic door before?' But that Watchman just looks at his shoes and leads the way, loans me his candle but won't come up. No-one will come up. They pretty much know what's there, I reckon, and though a public hanging is fun and games and a good day out, finding a rotten corpse right on your doorstep, so to speak, can't be enjoyed quite the same. Up the stairs I go with my candle, leaving the bottom door hanging off its hinges. It's quiet and eerie with the boot-trees swinging on their hooks, stale air stirring as I walk by. The attic door opens onto a wrinkle of stairs, well-worn and slightly spattered. Blood, I'm thinking, smelling rotten black puddings, and maybe the Watchman was right in staying his distance downstairs. And then there he is, the boot-tree man. Still with his big leather apron on and a wooden mallet by his side. He must've frozen solid these last few weeks, and is just beginning to melt, puddling the wood, head to one side, oozing. I'm going to need more than the two sacks I've brought, so I shouts down the stairs to fetch a few more from the baker's, and a flour shovel too. I look around while I wait, lighting the lanterns dangling from the beams. The room is long and wide, spread across the three houses. It has low tables, eight or nine, set with games and cards. There is chess and backgammon, Foxy-Run, Chase-the-Goose. Or almost, but the pictures on the board are different, lewd. A bit obscene, as are the carved pins on the table-skittles. At the chandler's end is a large low bed, and two bonnets hung on a set of hooks and a large cape. By the door stand two pairs of boots and some slippers. On a chair is a pair of trousers ripped at the back and badly stitched where someone has tried to mend them up with a rusty needle and a bobbin of old thread. The windows are boarded, except for the one over the baker's where the planks have been torn away. An old winch-hook sticks its black tongue from out the wall; in its elbow a knot of rope, which creeps over the sill and dangles its foot into darkness.

We figured out the story in the end, me, the doctor and the priest. After the boot-tree man had been found, a couple of people finally came forward and confessed that his attic had been used as a gaming house. There were straightforward games and some more specialised; there was alcohol and laudanum and opium at special request. Girls could be provided if ordered a few days in advance. Members arrived before the boot-tree man closed up shop at ten, and were obliged to stay the whole night, only leaving once he'd opened again in the morning. So neighbours saw nothing suspicious, and heard nothing because generally there was nothing to hear. All the clientele were of good breeding, the girls were clean, and carousing was kept to a minimum. The baker rarely heard anything more than a few foot-falls, but then he got up just gone midnight and spent the rest of the night in the baking cellar. The chandler never heard anything – he'd married Miss Twixley five years back and moved into her house on Dark Street, leaving his shop on the dot of eight every night. How the bishop got involved was a bit murkier, but it seemed he'd been a chess fanatic since a long time, and played regularly at the Nightingale Chess Café. That was until the archbishop put a stop to it. He'd said it was a Chinese war-game, and was as wicked and heathen as they were. They'd crucified missionaries, for God's sake! It was well known that the archbishop was mad as a mongoose and due to be popped in a box and dropped in the earth at any moment, but until that happened, he was still the boss, and what the archbishop forbade, to the bishop was forbidden. Rumours reached the bishop of the boot-tree man's club, and it was an easy matter to arrange to have his boots measured for trees. And so it had started. Under duress, and against church orders, the coachman confessed that he took the bishop every Thursday night to a place on Lime Road and picked him up at eight the next morning. The bishop was always muffled in a large cape, presumably to hide the fact that his clerical garb had been replaced by street clothing, and the insignia of his office removed.

'But it was Thursday when the body was found,' queried the doctor. 'Had he changed his routine? And if so, why?'

The minister, sighing over his tot of rum-and-tea, enlightened him: 'That week was the dedication of St Martin of Tours down at Wickham. The bishop would have had to travel on Thursday to be there for the saint's day, and stay on Friday for the consecration. His coachman said the bishop suddenly decided on Wednesday evening that he had to go out. That was the last he saw of him.'

We had patched together this tale of ours from interesting

bits and bobs of gossip, from the doctor's examinations of the two bodies and from the priest's internal sources. It seemed the bishop arrived at the boot-tree man's unannounced on Wednesday. We have to assume that the shop door was open and that the bishop went up. There he found the place deserted, apart from the boot-tree man lying dead on the attic floor. We none of us believed the bishop killed him, rather that he had got into a row with one of his regular girls and that she had lashed out and stabbed him in the neck with a long hat-pin. This we surmised because the doctor found the pearl-pointed pin buried in the boot-tree man's neck, going on an upward trajectory that would undoubtedly have pierced his brain, presumably with fatal results. The bishop had been a good man, despite his unfortunate obsession with chess, and had been stricken by his conscience. Should he report the man's death and hope the murderer could be found? Or would he be accused of the murder? Could he report it anonymously, or would even that lead to everyone finding out about the gaming club – and thus, indirectly, to his involvement in it? That would surely mean he would be disgraced and defrocked. However his mind worked, and no doubt it was swift and logical as befits a master chess player, he hit upon a third course and snuck out to the church. Knowing the layout, he went straight up to the gallery, sliced through the bell cord with a sharp knife he would've found in the boot-tree man's workshop, and returned to the scene.

Somewhere en route back to Pigeon Wynd he had been attacked by a dog. Or rather, the sugar-importer's ex-watchdog. The man had turfed the animal out on the street as useless because it persistently nipped his customers and couldn't seem to bark, only whine. The dog claimed the area round the church as his and it was later remarked by many that the dog had indeed been missing, if not mourned, this last month. What we decided was that the dog had followed the bishop with the rope tucked under his cape. Perhaps he gave it a tid-bit; perhaps the dog just followed him. Whatever, at some point it must have bitten the bishop, attested to both by the presence of the ripped trousers in the attic and by the pronounced bruising on the back of the bishop's thighs and buttocks, as seen by the doctor post-mortem. The dog must have still been gripping the bishop by the butt when he got to the shop, and maybe the bishop went in, took the mallet and gave it a whack to make it open its jaws. The baker had heard the dog whining at some point when he was lying in his bed. It seems that the bishop was a tidy man, and perhaps he decided to do one last good deed and rid the neighbourhood of a nuisance. One way or the other, the dog went flying out the window first. Maybe the bishop wanted to gauge the depth of the drop, or to make sure nothing was below that would impede his fall. He haphazardly tried to mend his trousers, but perhaps the dead man put him off, or he wasn't very adept at sewing, or he decided in the end that it just didn't matter. So he tied the rope around his neck – the knot was unusual, as I had noted before, and it turns out the bishop was a fisherman, and had used the exact same knot he used to tie a fly to a hook – and out he went. What must it have been like, leaping through that hatchment into Purgatory – for surely that is where he'd go? A good man he may have been, but suicide is a mortal sin and well he knew it.

'I'll have masses said, of course,' sighed the priest. 'I'm sure many of us will, although I doubt we'll be able to do them publicly. But he was a virtuous man, and if we can lessen the length of his suffering then we will.'

I could've added more to the tale at this point, but I like to keep myself private. I'd had a visit one morning from a young lady. She wore a bonnet very like the one hanging in the attic, and a pearl-studded pin, though those are common enough. She asked about the boot-tree man, how he was when I'd found him and the like. She started to cry, said she was his niece, and that she hoped he hadn't suffered. I told her what the doctor said, that it must have been very quick on account of the lack of blood. She snuffled a bit at that and said that was good, although he was a rude man, said she, and a boor and very quick to temper. I said maybe he deserved his end at that and she smiled up at me. Such blue eyes! Such a smile! And then she began to cry in earnest and once she'd started she couldn't stop. It was for the man who went out the window, she said: such a horrible way to die, and for no reason. Although, by then, we both knew the reason very well.

'He was such a nice man,' she sobbed, 'very kind and very gentle. All he wanted to do was to play chess.'

It doesn't seem a hanging offence, playing chess, although I've hanged men for less to please their betters. I'd not hang her pretty throat, though, and I never said a word. We're stepping out next Sunday, me and Ellie, and I've a mind we'll be doing it a lot more. I think there's a bit of fun to be had there. As uncle always says, why not enjoy the soup before you move onto the meat? In my case, I'm thinking spicy soup followed by veal. Maybe at the same time. I'll buy her a present tomorrow to persuade her – go to the milliners down Gargle, get a long hat-pin, topped with a pearl. Maybe tell her a secret, like lovers do.

BP's Boys

Mafeking, 1900, May 12th and the town has been besieged for almost seven months. Sergeant Major Goodyear of the Cadet Corps, 12 years old, pedals madly through lines of enemy fire carrying messages and what little supplies are left. He prefers the bicycle to the donkeys: faster, more manoeuvrable. The downside is you can't eat bicycles and food is getting very short. He tries not to worry, concentrates on weaving around potholes and unexploded munitions. He doesn't know it, but this is the last big assault before reinforcements finally arrive. B-P, the Commanding Officer, has held back troops nine times the size of his own for two hundred and seventeen days, and in a few short days Mafeking will be won.

Kimski Gopnik thinks of Goodyear and his dead donkeys while he sits shivering in the lee of a fallen tree. It is cold but, oddly, thunderclouds have gathered over the mountains and lightning shrieks from peak to peak. His dog Smiv was so frightened that she has run off into the trees. Half an hour ago they heard the shot whistling through the cold air, heard the brief bark of protest. Kimski tries to stop the tears, freezes his face with snow. He knows what will happen now. The snow covered their tracks as they went, but now little Smivka has given them all away. The soldiers will follow her tracks through the forest and find them. The stronger ones have gone ahead, are going to try to reach the gorge, drop down into the caves that line its sides. The younger ones, like Kimski, have volunteered to stay behind, to sweep over footmarks, crack branches, make false trails, try to melt back into the trees and down to the town before they are spotted. But for Kimski it is too late. He has twisted his knee and has nowhere else to go. He has whistled the alert, but knows no-one will reach him in time. He thinks of his mother, closes his eyes, tries to feel the warmth of her kitchen, smell the bread rising as she grinds up poppy-seeds, tells him how proud she is that he has joined the Cubs.

'Just like your father,' she says and sighs, wipes her hair away with the back of her hand, grinds the pestle a little harder.

And like his father, Kimski too will soon be dead.

Abaft, abeam, adrift, astern, haul the warp from the weatherside, and carry away. You could drown a man in the linguistic undercurrent of boats. Right now their rhythm gives me comfort, and I try not to think what is happening below. Six blasts on the whistle and we know someone is in trouble. The thunder has closed the sky over us like a box; the lightning is so close the air is crackling and our skin tingles as it splits the air, sends shockwaves gliding over the surface of the snow. We're in the hills of the Nizke Tatry trying to reach the river at Spisska Nova Ves. The Hitler Jugend have been tracking us ever since we left Bystrica. We didn't think they were so close. But haven't they always been close? Wasn't Caĉek, their leader, at school with me? He always came in crumpled clothes and only ever wore one sock. He never told us why. Look at him now! All shiny in his uniform, just like the ones we used to wear, exactly the same ones we used to wear. We were all together then, proud of our hats and our badges, happy to shout out that we were the Scouts of Zvolenka, worked hard for the honour it gave us. And then came 1939, and our country was carved up like a chicken and handed out on other people's plates. Midnight, and as the clocks of Munich chime, the men around the table pen their names to the paper. The Germans are there, and the Italians, the English, the French. But where are the Czechs? They are not represented at their own autopsy, and as September 29th slips in, we are hacked in two. If you axe a man off at the knees, the rest of him will soon fall. And so it was with us.

We've been trekking through these mountains all our lives, making camps and tying knots, setting traps, learning the names of trees and plants and the berries you can eat and those you can't, making canoes and paddles out of hand-sawn planks, learning to box the compass and follow the stars at night. Now our uniforms have been confiscated and our huts occupied by the Jugend. Several of our Scoutmasters have been shot for insurgency. Others have managed to survive out in the woods, on the hills, in caves. We have brought them food and clothing. We have passed messages between them, formed contacts with the Partisan Alliance, kept clear the escape routes that will lead them over the border into Russia and finally to join the exiled government of Beneŝ in London.

I am running through the thin snow, my boots skidding on the frozen pine needles beneath. My breath comes short and hard, the air getting too cold to be comfortable in my lungs. We have gone past the gorge and lowered the men by rope and gaffe. We have brushed the ground at the lip; disguised the scuffle by overlaying tracks of wolf and bear which we have stamped in wood. We have caught and killed a small deer, sprayed its blood in an arc through the trees. Now we are slipping away like fish down a salmon ladder, separating, keeping to shadows and undergrowth. I can hear them, the Jugend, crashing up the path we have just left. The cramp in my side makes me stop, doubles me over. I lean against a tree gasping for air, the cold bark melting snow into my back. Thunder growls overhead, knocks shivers of ice from my hat onto the hands I have braced against my knees. Just one more minute, I think, planning my route. I will speed my ascent, go up instead of down. I will go through the pass that will take me down to Brezno, I will...

Two strong bare hands have taken hold of my arms, forced them behind my shoulder-blades, sent me stumbling forward, my face hitting the frost-hard snow. My nose breaks with a crack and blood is forced through my mouth, gagging out dark and thick around my head. My hat has fallen off and someone grabs me by the hair, drags at my head, stretches the skin across my throat. I see two snow-sodden boots, one sock.

'He died today, your Baden-Powell. Did you know?'

He laughs, puts the blade of his knife under my chin, whispers in my ear, 'Somewhere in Africa, so I heard. Not much use to you now, eh?'

This isn't like Mafeking, where the young scouts led their prisoners happily through the town and everybody cheered and laughed. This time the prisoners are trussed in a line and stumbled through the High Street, past the Scout Tower where we hid a man for seven days. Horrified, people stand in their doorways, holding scarves to their mouths. Men come out of shops and cafés, brandishing the cutlery with which they had been eating. Someone shouts, 'But they're only boys!' and people are running on ahead to our houses, fetching out our fathers, if we have them, or our mothers, but the soldiers don't stop their procession. They take us to the field behind the bakery where the ground is slightly softer from the warmth of the ovens. Last summer it was stanchioned with sunflowers straining up towards the deep blue of the sky. Now it is dirty and bare, roughly run over with a plough. We are thrown shovels, told to dig. We dig, trying not to understand. Behind the low hedges and the circle of soldiers who stand by the gate, families shove and cry and wail and shout out our names – but no-one answers. Too soon, the hole is deep enough, although we went as slowly as we could. Too soon, the blood has dried hard as barnacles in my nose. Too soon, the tears have frozen on my face, on all our faces. There are five of us. We have a combined age of sixty-one. Bèla and Rudi whimper like abandoned kittens. I can see Bèla's grandmother, white-faced, crushed against the gate, clawing at a soldier who laughingly bats her off with his strong potato-pulling hands. I stare at the shovel as the soldier tells us to hand them back. I hold Jana's hand and he holds Jacov's. Together we stand, silently scanning for the faces we want most to see. Then the Commander gives the order and the Jugend lift their rifles. My heart jumps within me like a rat trying to escape a hole. I cannot find my mother though I look and look, and Jana is squeezing so tightly the bones in my hand begin to break, the thunder still murmurs high in the mountains and I hear a buzzard keen in the rising wind and I feel the pinch of the cold air on my cheeks and without closing my eyes I –

Five small bodies crumple backwards into the dark grave and

the sound of the bullets echoes in a silence that will hang for a long time over the baker's field. People weep at the hedge and the soldiers put down their guns and slowly start shovelling the hard earth back into the hole.

'Let this be a warning to you all...' shouts the voice of a boy they thought they knew, until he turned into a man. He wears two boots, his one sock hidden by his trousers, but already the crowd have closed their ears and are helping away those who cannot stand with the sudden, shocking grief of it all.

Up on the mountain, Kimski has crawled down the hill and found the body of his dog. He has cleaned her up with fistfuls of snow and moss and hung his whistle around her neck. He has leant his head upon the cold fur, curled himself up from the world and gone to sleep. No-one will find him and he will stay on the mountain forever.

Sunrise hits the gorge late, and the snarl of wolves at its lips have taken the deer and dragged it deep into the wood. A gaffe appears, catches at the hard earth. Three men pull themselves up and over and start across the hills on the long trek down to Spisska. Two of them will make it over the border; one of them will manage to reach England and sign up with the Czech Air Force Reserves. He will be downed over Dresden and will never visit the graves of the boys shot dead in the baker's field of Zvolenka in 1941.

JACOV FIALKA	WHO DIED AT THE AGE OF 12
KAREL GOLDBERG	WHO DIED AT THE AGE OF 15
BÈLA GRINKOP	WHO DIED AT THE AGE OF 13
JENA JANACEK	WHO DIED AT THE AGE OF 13
RUDI MYSHTEK	WHO DIED AT THE AGE OF 8

WHO DIED IN THE SERVICE OF THEIR COUNTRY
& UPHELD THE SCOUTING LAW

REMIS VELISQUE: THEY TOO GAVE OF THEIR BEST.

Note: *the Scout Movement, as founded by Baden-Powell, was very active in Czechoslovakia right up to the outbreak of the Second World War. Although not actively discouraged, many of the activities and areas in which the Scout Troops operated were absorbed into the Hitler Youth, who appropriated their uniforms and huts and organisation. Many of the Underground Leaders were former Scouts, and the code of conduct of Scouts led them to act as messengers and suppliers. Many hundreds died, not only in Czechoslovakia but all over Europe, carrying out these duties, tortured, shut away in concentration camps, or shot, hands bound behind them with barbed wire. Some are recorded as being as young as seven.*

Across the Azov

Joab lies drowned in the Putrid Sea where we left him last summer season. It's a noxious place: swamps of weed and fart-stinking gas, but the wild-fowling's good. Which is why we go there. That year we'd got three casks of bittern which we'd salted down; two barrel of eel, widgeon and teal and swan, and another one of marten. The spit of land we call the Arabat Tongue keeps the lagoon from the Azov Sea, and along its length we kept the fires going, damped with green rushes so the smoke would choke the mosquitoes. It also cured the fish we caught and split and strung between the willows, and when we weren't hunting, we wove withies into baskets to carry the smokies home.

Our village is at the top of the Azov, across the bay from Taganrog where we've a cousin will take five or six of us in his boat. Every midsummer we have a dance and a drink and wait for the winds to come. It sweeps across the steppes from the east and blows so hard the water pulls back across the bay and leaves fourteen miles of sand from here to the boatyard. We don't know exactly when it will come but it always does, so we watch our frog-jars. They're leaf-green and hard to see, but when the weather is fine they climb the twigs and blink in the sun, slap at the flies stuck on the honey-smeared lid. Their skin puckers with the approaching storm and down they go under weed and water to wait. That's when we know the wind is on its way and away goes the vodka, locked in its cupboard, and the spruce-beer back to the pantry. We oil our boots and check our splatchers – the wickerwork skis we use to slide across the mud. We drain the samovars and pack our bags with clothes, blankets, bread and knives, and those who have guns check barrels and powder and shot. Then we lie on our backs on the sand-shoals of the Azov and gaze over to the east. The horizon shimmers in the clear blue skies and still we wait.

There's always one frog goes down first, head tucked, feet

suckered against the stems. The rest cock their heads, blow bubbles in their pea-green throats, make odd, uneasy croaks. We shade our eyes and stare at the sky. A faint grey wisp begins to gather just as the sun is setting. One by one the frogs descend as a bank of cloud begins to roll across the steppe. By dawn the windows rattle and it's hard to breathe outside for the sand and dust. We strap our bags onto our backs and our wickers onto our feet. The wind rampages and it's hard to stand but the waves have rolled back and ten of us set out across the mud. Within minutes we've lost sight of the village and it's hard to see each other's backs, but the wind pushes us on in the right direction. It's always the right direction: it hasn't changed for a hundred years. All we can hear is the mud sucking at our splatchers, and the occasional grunt as someone goes over, and the whine of the wind in our ears. It's a hard four hours' work to get across the flats, all the time hoping the winds won't drop because then the water will come flooding back and sweep us away on the bore. We go in twos in case of accident – the sand can sink away below your feet and it's no use struggling. You've to lie still and wait for your mate to pull you out, or crawl slowly to the solids and drag yourself up, hoping your boots and splatchers are still attached to your feet. I'm with Alexander and we're pushing to get ahead. Only the first of us get on the boat and two months of money and work. The rest trek back home on the land-side of the bay, which isn't so bad. A couple of days ambling, maybe a few drinks. The worst of it is reaching home and seeing the disappointment on your family's faces, listen to the words:

'Never mind... It can't be helped... There's always next year... Maybe if you trained a little beforehand... At least the mud didn't take you and you didn't drown...'

When I was ten and he was eight, me and Leo strapped boards to our feet and tried to follow across the sand. We got ten yards before we sank. We screamed and laughed; got frightened when the mud reached our knees and we couldn't get out.

'Pieter!' wailed my brother and I could see his arms flailing as he struggled and tried to pull up his feet.

'Hold still!' I yelled, the wind filling my mouth with sand. My heart beat like the devil, but I did what I'd been taught: leaned over, brought the boards up by the strings attached to my heels, my fingers finding the knots looped at my shoulders as I pulled, felt the tug on my boot as my knee bent back, and up it came, board and all. The hardness in my throat turned to exhilaration as I got my balance and slid towards my brother.

'I'm sinking!' he cried, his face white as tallow. 'Pieter, I'm sinking!'

'No you're not, you baby,' I laughed and took a hold of his hands. 'Come on. Let's get you up.'

Five minutes later we were cowered in a cove on the shore, sheltering from the wind.

'You only went up to your knees,' I poked little Lyovushka in the ribs and pulled his hat over his eyes.

'So did you too!' he protested, and whacked my leg with his bag.

We'd made a fire of the boards and dug up some cockles which were sizzling away in the embers.

'We'll make proper ones next time,' I said. 'Big long ones like Dad's used to be.'

'Will you make me some too?' asked Lyovushka. 'Just like Dad's?'

'Just like Dad's,' I agreed.

'And next year we'll go all the way over?'

'You and me,' I promised, 'all the way.'

Lyovushka smiled and gave me a handful of cockles burnt hard as nuts and tasting of ash. When we got home we were covered in cinders and sand and mother made us strip and wash in front of the fire. She rubbed us down with handfuls of hay, wrapped us in eiderdowns, fed us potatoes and butter-cake.

'We must have gone at least a mile, didn't we Pieter?' boasted Lyovushka, while mother ruffled his hair, pulled the quilt tight around him.

'Easily,' said I, winking at mother who was smiling and glad to have us home. 'Maybe even two.'

But I knew how far I got that first time, and I swore next

time I'd get right over. And I spent two years getting my wicker splatchers woven, and another year practising. And then I did get over, and the next year I took Leo, just like I'd promised that day in the cove. And then me and Alexander won the race. It was the hardest thing I'd ever done, straining through the grit and sand, legs aching, calf-muscles splitting, pushing ourselves further using poles. And then the boatmen were cheering us in and telling us we were first! The wind was fierce as hell as we fought towards the makeshift tent below the stanchions of the pier. Wiry arms pulled us into shelter, pushed back our scarves and hats, undid the wattles from our feet, force-fed us the vodka and tea that had been warming on the stove. Half an hour and in crawled Andrew and Grigor, whooping and hooraying; more vodka and tea; more backslapping and stories. Then Chrystos and Boris blew in and they'd to toss a coin to see who would stay with the boat-crew and who had to go home. The five of us were carried off to the boat to drink more vodka and thank God we didn't have to leave till the wind had dropped and we'd had a bit of time to sober up. The second the wind was down and the water was back in, up went the sails and away went the crew, racing on the back of the bore as it hit the shore and rebounded. I was so excited and still a bit drunk, helping get the tackle ready, brewing tea, stacking the barrels. I never thought to ask, when did Leo come in? Did he come last? Did anybody see? But nobody had seen. And mother and me, we never saw our little Lyovushka again.

The fog was cruel, thick along the Tongue, come creeping from the swamp to the sea. Couldn't see in front of you, couldn't see behind. Couldn't see the fish-strings a yard above the fire. There's nothing we could do – soon as we saw it sneaking through the osiers, under the lichen and the old man's beard, we set the traps and nets and went back to camp; got aboard the boat. My boat. It's twenty years on since I first went on the boats to Arabat. I've worked hard; I've saved. I've bought a little house in Taganrog – only two rooms, but there's only me. Mother went three years after Leo sank himself in the race across the sands. Times have changed – our village has no work, and this year all the men are racing across the sands to get first to the boats and what little work there is. I take on the first seven who get here. Joab came in sixth. He's out of breath and the first thing he does when he reaches the pier is roll a cigarette in shaking hands. The Mendel brothers come in soon after and mutter about being tripped – saying someone dropped branches in their path; casting dark looks at Joab. But I stick to my guns and I tell the Mendels: who takes branches all the way over the sands just to trip someone up? Who would go to the bother? Just like always, I take whoever comes in first. They've always been the rules and I'm not going to be the one to break them.

The fog is so thick you can feel it in your throat. It lies for two days while we stay in our bunks playing cards, drinking. Every few hours, someone goes out to check the traps and reset them. We skin the catch and salt them down in their barrels, clean the pelts, disinfect the feathers to rid them of lice and ticks. It's Joab's turn out and he's been a while. The boys are settled into a game of poker, so I volunteer to go and check. Out I go and the fog is green amongst the trees. I can hear the water whisper on the Tongue. I walk by the dark mounds of cinders, smell the damp smoke, feel its tar on my face. Joab is sat by the marten traps; he's found the bottle of vodka I put in his pocket. It's almost empty and he's lying on his back, his cigarette smouldering in his hand. He's not quite passed out, but his words are slurred and he gropes to find the bottle, grabs it by the neck and shakes it at me. I take a quick slug, pass it back, sit on the bank above him, gaze down into the ripple of the stinking swamps.

'Check the traps, Joab?'

He slaps the bulging sack by his feet, 'Checked 'em,' he says and puts the bottle to his lips, empties it, throws it into the swamp. We barely hear the splash as it sinks into the roots and heavy green water.

'You never told me about Leo,' I say, and he rolls his head on his wobbling neck, trying to look up at me.

'Years ago,' he mumbles. 'No time. You know that. Couldn't do nothing for him. You know that.'

He's repeated the story many times, about how Lyovushka hit a pocket of wet sand, went up to his waist in a second. That by the time he called out, Joab was too late and couldn't pull him out. How he ran on as fast as he could to get help. How he'd come in seventh and nearly made the boat. How they'd gone back for Leo but it was all too late, and we never found his body or bones or boots or knapsack or splatchers. How we never found anything of Lyovushka ever again.

I give Joab a hard kick in the back and watch him rolling down the bank, hands adrift, the red stub of his cigarette still in his mouth. He looks surprised and puzzled. I slide down the bank and watch as he sinks into the thick swamp pool, see him grasping at the edge. I kick his fingers away from the bank.

'You left my Leo,' I say, speaking quiet. 'You should have stayed and pulled him out. At least you should have stayed. A boy shouldn't die like that alone.'

There's a huge lump in my throat and no more words will come. I lean back into the damp and drip of the reeds and hear Joab thrashing in the water, waiting for the roots to catch his feet and the dark weed to wrap around his body and drag him down. A billow of fog rolls out from the foetid trees and wipes away the noise, fills my ears. I crawl back up the bank and sit by the embers of the fire, waiting. Listening. All I hear is my own breathing, so I stand, and work my way back to the boat. He left my Leo, and twenty years too late, I've left him. Let him take his chances. Let him be alone. God knows, I am. Strangely, I feel taller, older, I've the taste of burnt cockles in my mouth, feel the splatcher-boards under my feet, the wet sand on my ankles, the wind in my face.

'Well?' say the boys when I roll onto my bunk.

'No sign,' I say. 'Just an empty bottle.'

'Thieving bastard,' says Chrystos, taking two cards from the deck.

'Give him an hour,' says Alexander, 'then we'll look again.'

'Mist might've lifted by then,' adds Grigor. 'Did it look like it was lifting?'

I've turned my back on them, pulled a blanket up around my shoulders, kicked off my boots.

'Might lift by morning,' I offer. 'Things always look better in the morning.'

Not for Joab they didn't, who never saw another one, and who's still lying abandoned of his life in the Putrid Sea. The mist did rise, but slowly, slowly, and though me and the boys looked, we never found a sign of him. Only his bag of catch and a vodka bottle choked up with the mud of the Tongue.

Of Phlegraean Fields

My first meeting with Ettore Sigliano required that I take him for an imbecile, going around as he did with his arm held up in front of his face with only the tips of his eyelashes showing. This practice he pursued even whilst eating, which could only be managed through a long straw or by placing the ends of oil-soaked spaghetti directly into his mouth. It was not an engaging habit, and there were other things too. One could not help but remark on his clothing, for example. Below the waist he wore breeches and boots as normal; above was a shirt of violent blue which was missing a sleeve and was pinned above one shoulder by a large pearl brooch. Any one of these latter points would have raised suspicion, but worst was the large stained bandage about his raised arm, which was inexpertly tied and left lines of hair protruding from the wrappings to blow in the winter wind. I found it incomprehensible that a man of his reputation should have become a lunatic in the two months it had taken me to travel here.

We had been corresponding on the construction of my Mirratory, a room whose every surface was to be covered in mirrors, including ceiling, floor and furniture. A small fountain would play at the centre, and from strategically placed lanterns, scenes of mountain and meadow were to be projected. It was to be the perfect place of peace for the convalescent, or those who merely wished to escape the outside world for an hour or two. I had hopes that it might be adopted both as therapy and entertainment, and had invested a considerable amount in the project. I had come to the Bay of Naples to meet the man who was considered the finest mirror-maker in Europe and discuss with him the final specifications for my plans. I had not come all this way to entertain a fool.

'Only another two days, Signor Hoxby, and then this ... this ... this *monstrous* proboscis will be gone.'

Ettore Sigliano sighed as I poured him more coffee and patted the arm that rested on the table. The other was still sewn to his face, his nose buried in the crook of his elbow. I had discovered that far from being an idiot, Ettore was in fact undergoing a complicated surgical procedure which I am not sure I would have had the stomach to endure. Two weeks before my arrival, he had had the bad luck of having an explosion in his workshop through no fault of his own. Some of the chemicals he had been using to give colour and strength to the glass were of recent invention, and their properties little understood. Leaving them percolating gently through a double-bellied still, Ettore had gone off to mix more pigment. Meanwhile his neighbour, who used their combined roof to raise his pigeons, had removed the shield from the skylight to scrape off the droppings and weed-sprouts that had collected there. The sun was strong that day, despite the general chilliness of the weather, and the dimples in the skylight concentrated the light and forced several heated beams down upon the still. The extra warmth was enough to overheat the catalyst which caused a chain reaction, ultimately blowing the entire apparatus apart. Splinters and shards of glass were hurled through the air, and it was one of these latter that had sliced Ettore's nose clean off.

Hence the arm. He was following the instructions given in the famous surgical manual of Gaspare Tagliacozzi, whose name means 'mussel-cutter', an amusing homonym to my English ears. This procedure required a flap of skin to be excised from the forearm and sewn to the remnants of the nose whilst still attached to the arm, thereby ensuring adequate blood supply. After a minimum of fourteen days, assuming the graft had taken and not turned gangrenous, the join was cut and the remaindered skin stretched and moulded into shape. This latter stage would take a further three months. I stupidly inquired why he didn't just attach the original nose – after all, such accidental amputation is a rare but not unknown occurrence in a glass-maker's shop, and such cuts are generally clean. The usual procedure is to retrieve the severed finger/toe/ear/nose, rinse it in alcohol, and sew it back on as best one can. In reply I was told that the explosion had taken out most of the inside of the laboratory, including the doors and an adjoining wall. The skylight was blown clean out of its putty and found the next day, astoundingly still intact, in the mud-bath of Aldina Dioscorides' pigs. It was assumed that the nose had been projected on a similar journey, or that some crow had pilfered it from the mess and away to its nest. Crow-crop or pig's gullet – either way, the nose God gave Ettore Sigliano was not to be found in the charred debris of the workshop and, it seems, was gone for good.

Hoping to entertain his guest and take his mind off the significant pain his graft was giving him, Ettore offered to take me to the Burning Plains of Campania, which place the Greeks ('a superstitious bunch,' volunteered Ettore) believed to contain the entrance to Hell. We passed first through terraces of pink apricots and almonds, sea-green deeps of fennel, beans and peas. But every yard we drew closer, the herbage yellowed, the sulphurous stench increased, and soon we were tying napkins around our faces. Ettore was already draped about the muzzle with a bandage and a protective guard fashioned from some light metal buckled around the back with a leather strap. I doubted he could smell anything, but even he could taste the bitter cinders that were everywhere in the air. Our clothes and horses became covered in a light grey drift that seemed dry to the touch but stuck like glue. Whatever Ettore's opinion of the Greeks, there was no doubting they were right about the Phlegraei Campi. I have been to many places, but none compare: the entire area was desolate of green and lay strewn with barren rock, much as one sees the moon through a telescope. We were the only living things who passed across the face of the plain, apart from the eccrisis sputtered from the cluster of underground volcanoes which simmered below our feet. There were caves filled with choking gas, a labyrinth of smoking crevices, fissures which seemed to drop to the bottom of the earth. The very ground smouldered its warmth into the leather of our boots, which Ettore had rightly insisted be stout and well-nailed. He and his manservant were a little way behind, putting some adjustments to the buckle and trying to fix a cover for his eyes which were streaming and looking very inflamed.

I had gone on a little, to investigate a small mound which rose from the flat level of the plain and, startling in this monoscape, appeared streaked with yellow and red. I approached with caution, for it could have been with heat that it was coloured, a vomit of molten lava perhaps, or a cauldron of red-hot pumice. The immediate horror of my recognition made me gag and I started so violently that my horse shied and threw me to the ground. At that very moment, I heard a hiss as of a hundred snakes, and a roaring of water in my ears. My horse bolted across the plain, tripped and disappeared down a smouldering crevasse. I turned to confront the noise and saw a geyser spume a boil of yellow water over Ettore and his man. Bernardo had tried to protect his master and was even now dragging him from the edge of the simmering pool, but a splatter of hot ash still fell on them both, spattering their clothes with pocks and burns. Worse for Ettore, his makeshift mask had been removed as Bernardo adjusted the straps, and we could smell the scorch of new-born skin as the searing shower hit. Without a doubt one could tell that all was ruined, and Ettore fell to the ground, his hands covering his face, blood and tears of pain seeping through his fingers, criss-crossing the grey of his skin like a caravan of Bedouin trails through the scorch of desert sands.

You may or may not have guessed that my dogged pursuit of the Mirratory is primarily for medical gain. It is true that I am a student of the mind rather than the body, but to treat one you must sometimes treat the other. Because of this, I have studied the rudimentary texts of anatomy and physiology and felt obliged to examine the wreck of Ettore's face. The skin had fallen back into his nasal cavity and was smoking slightly where the edges melted. Without wasting a second I leapt to my feet and ran to where I had left my pack. Grabbing the geological hammer I had brought with me, I sprinted to the fallen figure I had earlier discovered. It was not unlike one of the bodies one finds at Pompeii or Herculaneum – although much more recent, and it was obviously that of some poor traveller overcome by a larger pyroclastic display than the one which had engulfed

my companions. Clasping the handle hard so that I should not
lose my nerve, trying to think of a quiet evening's golf when
all rests on the final putt on the green, I swung the hammer.
Running back to Ettore I forced him to sit up, shouting at
Bernardo in execrable Italian to hold his master firmly by the
shoulders. This done, and with no time to waste, I turned the
object in my hand to the right elevation and jammed it hard
into Ettore's face. He had been ready for it, but still his scream
made my heart shudder and Bernardo began to cry. Even so, I
held the dead man's nose in place. It was a desperate measure,
but God knows what He takes and knows what He gives and
in this case, He chose to give. The petrified appendage sealed
the wound, and saved Ettore a further measure of his already
sadly depleted face.

I am lying in my Mirratory, sunk deep into my bed, listening as
the fountain plays in its pool. We have made our fortune, Ettore
and I, and soon there will be one in every city across Europe.
It turns out that my heroic contribution to nasal surgery was
slight, the Phlegraean prosthetic detaching itself after only
a week. It did, however, give Ettore one last idea, and he
fashioned for himself a nose out of ochre-tinted glass, nostrils
and all. The agonies he suffered cauterising his already raw
wound and incorporating his new nose do not bear thinking
about. I for one would rather have buckled an iron shoe to my
face in the manner of Tycho Brahe, who lost his nose in a duel,
poignantly for neither a woman nor the honour of his family,
but to argue a point in mathematics. One has to wonder what
brought him to such a pass. He would have benefited, as Ettore
does now, from an hour or two in the Mirratory.

There is one unusual event which occurred about six months
after the incidents I have described. Signora Dioscorides' son
became a local celebrity and ultimately joined a travelling fair
which passed through the town. His act consisted of "Hector
The Amazing Pig," who could apparently sniff out a plate
of oil-soaked spaghetti from wherever you hid it in a room.
You could even bury it in a box a foot underground, a feat
I witnessed for myself. There are experiments one could do,

of course, but it would involve divesting Ettore of yet more body parts – and somehow, after what he has gone through, I doubt he would agree. Instead, Gaspare Dioscorides and Hector travel the booths of Europe ingesting far more spaghetti than is good for either of them.

I have been back to the Phlegraean Fields on many occasions, and now sell pumice-powder as a medicinal poultice. I offered Ettore some credit for the discovery, but he has declined. He prefers to stay at home and polish his new glass noses, of which he now has an impressive few. He has even had several commissions: one from a soldier who lost his nose to the Napoleonic Scourge; two more from duellists, neither of whom knew the first thing about mathematics. There was also one made for a young lady who had hated her own, rather large, nose so much that she had employed a surgeon to taper it down a bit. The procedure had worked, but the stitches became septic and after a while her retrousséd flesh dissolved away in a drip of green pus.

As a consequence, she had not left her house for three years, and felt the warmth of the sun only in her enclosed garden. We developed a small cushioned clip which enabled her to adjoin her new noses to her remaining cartilage. She had spent her cloistered years absorbing book after book, and with her new nose was a fine catch for any man who valued rarity above beauty. She was married soon after, choosing to wear the amber nose, which had preserved within it the petal of a tiny rose. Ettore chose a pale cerise so as not to clash with his new bride. They were married in the large Mirratory we had opened in town, the lanterns swaying soft lights across the walls, the fountain waters dyed a delicate green. As bride and groom became man and wife they kissed, sending a chime as of toasting champagne glasses ringing through the hush of the room.

I still hear it today, as pure a sound as ever I have heard, and am proud to say I was a part of its creation.

Private Makar Makes Promotion

To make a fire, first find a man named Ostropovich and feed him vodka till he's drunk, but not so drunk he's unconscious. Set the table with candle, pen and paper and put Ostropovich in the chair you've dragged over from the old desk in the corner. Put the pen in his hand, start rambling about the good old days, then head to the kitchen to make coffee and leave by the back door. Try not to slip on the ice and break your ankle in the radish patch; try not to howl like a dog till Ostropovich comes stumbling out and drags you halfway up the steps till his back gives out and he leaves you to go and get help, then forgets you're there and gets back to the table and his interminable writing leaving you to freeze to death in the cold Siberian wind.

It was a simple plan. I'd been hand-picked from my unit to set up the sting. All through the summer, some unpatriotic wretch had been scribbling seditious poems and shoving them through people's letterboxes. Well, we called them poems because they didn't approximate to much else, and you know how pretentious these so-called writers are. Any old nonsense passes for poetry these days – it doesn't even have to rhyme or have a hero or a story. Here's one of the miscreant's better efforts, which is not saying much:

> Men *without words*
> *Are Men without hearts.*
> *Men without hearts*
> *Are animals.*

The streets were littered with this drivel where sensible-minded citizens had ejected them through the front door the moment they discovered them loitering on their mats with the Morning Message. The Message is our very own paper, produced in the barracks on a proper printing press, and has the right kind of writing that encourages the workers and doesn't get them all stirred up like that poetry trash. Even outside on the streets it continued to cause trouble – several people, including the Commander's wife, had slipped on them and cracked their elbows or shins when they fell. The Commander rightly concluded that the time for tolerance was over and that the menace must be stopped. Up until then, we'd regarded these epigrams as a prank and laughed about them over our morning porridge. How could you take seriously someone who wrote:

Should you swallow the sun as well as the moon?
Should your throw out your foot because the shoe's too
small?
Should you chop off your head because the hat doesn't
fit?

But when the Commander's wife ruined her coat and dropped her bag of cakes in a puddle because of this rubbish, it was time to put a stop to it. The Commander put up a huge poster on the side-wall of the baker's. It took us ages to print because we had to do it all in separate pages and then paste them all up in the right order to make one big message which read:

THE SCRIBBLER MUST BE STOPPED.
HE IS UNDERMINING THE ORDER OF THIS TOWN.
ANYONE HARBOURING THE SCRIBBLER WILL BE
PUNISHED.
ANYONE OFFERING INFORMATION AS TO HIS IDENTITY
WILL BE REWARDED.

Anyone who stood in the bread-queue (which is everyone in town) couldn't avoid reading the poster, so no-one had any excuses. Every morning for a week we went out to the baker's with our notebooks and interrogated everyone in the queue, one by one. There was a lot of grumbling because people kept losing their places while we were interviewing them, and on several occasions fist-fights broke out and baskets were broken over people's heads, but a few slaps with the baton and the odd pistol shot soon put an end to all that. Despite our efforts, we didn't get anything useful that week. There were lots of denunciations of course, but none of them came to anything, though obviously we kept a few accusees under lock and key to let the townspeople know that we knew our business. Still, some of the names we got were so preposterous, it was hardly worth our while going to check it out. Take Evinka Nagulnov: it was hard to imagine her creeping round the streets in the early hours of the morning pushing nonsense through people's letterboxes. Most nights she was over at the barracks keeping a few of the lads company, and just because her neighbours don't understand that to help a soldier is to help your country, there's no need to go blabbing to the authorities. We took her away for a few days just to show we weren't prejudiced and even the Commander gave her a stern talking to for well over half an hour.

At the end of the week, what we had was half a dozen notebooks stuffed with the same old statements. We even stopped writing them down after a while, just jotted down the citizen's name and said AEE – as everyone else. Everyone said that the poems just appeared on their doormats every now and then, or were tucked into the postholes of the communal flats. No-one saw anyone, not even the night-shift boys returning from the mines or the old tramp Konovienko who roamed around the dawn streets stringing up cats by their tails. This is strange behaviour I know, but he says that when he was in the camps during the war he collapsed in the potato fields and when he came to he found himself covered in cats who were nibbling at his face and fingers and had eaten away his boots. It's true that half his mouth is missing and that he's lost a few fingers and toes, but it is also true that he was in the camps during the war, which means he must be as unpatriotic as they come and is without doubt a liar. And besides, he stinks so badly of shit I doubt a starving rat would touch him, let alone a cat, although they are meat-eaters, and if the only other choice was potatoes frozen hard in their fields? Well, Konovienko was younger then. Maybe he didn't smell quite so bad in those days, and maybe those camp cats aren't so fussy. Or maybe he just got frostbite and dreamed the whole thing. Either way, there were constant complaints about him torturing the feline population and once a year we used to give him a good beating just to let him know we knew.

Well, all in all there were about a hundred and ten denunciations, most of which were anonymous and most of which proved groundless. Each unit covered five addresses a day and that way we finished the lot in a week. Anyone remotely suspicious was handcuffed and taken off to the barracks. The Commander was quite specific about what to look for: anyone who had too many books, particularly foreign ones; anyone who possessed a lot of pens and paper; anyone who had an illegal press in their basement. (This was a long-shot, though obviously whoever found one would hit the jackpot. No-one did.) Anyone who quoted anything vaguely poetical when accused of the crime; anyone whose boots seemed far too worn down; anyone who looked like they weren't getting enough sleep. If anyone fitted one of these criteria, they were deemed suspicious and were to be tied to a chair and interrogated. Anyone fitting two of these criteria (unless it was just the boots-and-tiredness thing, which fitted most of the populace of the town) was to be publicly carted off to the barracks and have a red cross painted on their doors so that neighbours would know to watch out for them. If three criteria fitted, we detained them and asked if they wanted to confess. Nothing seemed to work. We did get a few confessions, but even so, the Scribbler's notes were still arriving sporadically, and eventually, after cross-checking the nights that our suspects spent with us, and the nights the Scribbler was active, we had to let every last one of them go, although three of them left via the hospital, which just goes to show that you should never confess to anything that isn't true.

It left us in a rather awkward position, and the Commander was not pleased. The morning after the note which read –

> *Some cats catch mice*
> *Some cats don't;*
> *Some cats are so fat*
> *The mice can catch the cats*

– the Commander came stamping into the station, slapping everyone in sight and shouting at the top of his voice that there was a crate of vodka waiting – and the best vodka, not just the shit we get for everyday use – for the man who came up with a scheme to catch The Scribbler. He thumped the table so hard all the papers and the pen-box jumped off onto the floor, then he said we'd got two hours to come up with a scheme or we would all be sent for a two-week emergency stint at the retraining camp. We didn't need telling twice and we all starting talking and yelling and someone retrieved the pen-box and handed round papers and pencils and we got to work. There wasn't a huge variety of ideas that came out, but the Section Chief seemed fairly pleased with the results and took the best ones off to the Commander.

1.   *We could try patrolling again, though it hadn't worked last time. The Scribbler just waited until the patrol had moved on or picked a different district. One improvement on this would be to split the units up into individuals and stand them on the street corners. This might work, but then again it was putting the soldiers in danger. It is never safe for one soldier to be out on his own on the streets, especially after dark. There are always insurgents and rebels trying to wreck the order of the state in the person of the individual.*
2.   *Obviously, not everyone could compose poetry, even if it was the type of tripe doggerel the Scribbler enjoyed. We should check off everyone who has been a student or who carried on going to school after the statutory age of fourteen, after which respectable people went out and worked for their living instead of scrounging off the state and their fellow citizens.*
3.   *We could glue up all the letterboxes, although this would mean that the Morning Message couldn't be delivered either, which was the main source of inspiration and strong moral fibre our citizens had come to expect. They wouldn't take kindly to its sudden withdrawal and it might lead to adverse effects and a rise in crime.*

4.   *We could randomly interrogate one member of every family in the entire town until the guilty party confessed to save his loved ones from suffering further embarrassment and the possibility of pain and serious injury.*

Number 4 was the firm favourite with all of us, including the Section Chief; the only problem with it being that it would take too long, even with us all working double shifts, and also that some people had no family. We talked about using neighbours or work-mates or even pets instead of actual relaions, but the whole thing just got too complicated. So then we came up with a clever solution: we would work a combination. We would find firstly those who had been students or been to university; we would increase our watch on their areas; we would single out their families for surveillance and interrogation, then after a week we would collate a shortlist of suspects we could really go to work on. We would not be obvious about it – we didn't want the townspeople thinking the Scribbler was getting to us, that he was more important than he was. We wanted him disposed of quietly and without a fuss. We didn't want a martyr at the end of all this.

And so we got down to it. We ended up with fifteen names and then fifteen crack soldiers were selected, of which I am proud to say I was one. We were each given a name and a cover story. We put on our normal clothes and were each given a couple of litres of vodka and our instructions.

Off to Gogolov Square, turn left at the cobbler's, down the alley, second door on the right. It's painted a rather vile shade of green, which is suspicious in itself – it means the person who lives inside likes things a little different. He isn't content with the browns and blacks that everyone else has. He's going to have green and damn the harmony of the whole street. He's got a window box as well, though there's not much to see under the snow, just a bit of ivy straggling over the sides and what looks like the tops of two carrots. I hold the bottle-bag tight against my chest and knock on the door. We had to do a practice session in knocking – hammering is a dead give-away apparently, and the normal citizenry just tap their arrival and don't like waking the neighbours. Presumably this means that there's less bodies piling in to drink the vodka. I know from my own experience that thirsty peasants can smell free booze up to three streets away. Nobody comes at first, but I know the man is in because I've already checked the place out. The light in the pantry is dim but on and I saw him moving about earlier. I even saw him taking his piss-bucket out to water the vegetables. I knock again, a bit harder, but nothing intimidating. It's like a Morse code that's saying, *come on you old fart, it's frigging freezing out here*, and sure enough, I hear slippers shuffling down the hall. The bolt is pulled back and an eye stares out at me through a crack. It's a blue eye, covered in glass, and with the watery look we've been taught to associate with intellectuals. I slap on a smile and start to speak in a cheery voice.

'Maxim Ostropovich? It *is* Maxim Ostropovich isn't it? I know you don't know me but my name is Timofei. Timofei Damaskov. You knew my uncle when you taught at the State College.'

I could have added, *before you got thrown out for making trouble. Just because the staff hadn't been paid for two months is no need to go causing a riot. We should support the state in its hour of need, not kick it while it's down as if it were some dirty old dog.* The man says nothing, so I casually allow the two bottles to clink together in the bag and go on with my story. They really have been well researched, these stories of ours, and are a damn site better written than anything the Scribbler has come up with. We have deep background and everything. I tell Maxim Ostropovich I'm visiting the local copper mine, writing a paper for the University (a good one, but not the best – don't want to go overboard) on the working conditions of the miners and how they could be improved and that my uncle told me to look him up while I was in town. The door eventually opens a crack more and a whole face appears. Grey and sagging, a moustache stained yellow with tobacco, not much hair. I notice his fingers are stained with ink.

'I have vodka,' I say, thrusting the bag at him, starting to stamp my feet in the cold. And it really is cold, standing there on the step. The wind is whipping straight down my collar, which isn't nearly as good as our army ones which have fur on them, and we've got proper hats instead of this linen crap. Eventually the man Maxim opens the door and moves back to let me in. He hasn't asked to see my papers, which is a shame, because they're rather good. I've even got a photo on the University one, and it seems a shame to waste it. Maybe I'll give it to Evinka when next I see her.

'So who's your uncle?' he asks when we're finally sat at the table. He's got a tiny fire going in the grate, but the light from the gas lamp is rubbish. The whole room looks full of shadows and I get an awful fright when something jumps out of the corner and starts rubbing against my leg. A cat. Score one, I think, and there's a bookcase. Score two.

'Pavlov Kemper,' I answer. 'He used to teach Botany to the First Level students. He always spoke well of you and told me to look you up when I got to town.'

'Ah, ah,' said the man – I was about to say old man, but that is misleading. He looked old on immediate impression, but looking further, as we soldiers are trained to do, I could see that he was actually a good deal younger than first appeared. Of course I knew his age to be fifty-six – that was part of our research – but you can't ignore what's in front of your face.

Score three. Trying to disguise himself.

'Yes, Kemper. Pavlov Kemper, I remember him. Though I didn't know him well. I'm surprised he remembers me at all; we rarely met, with him being in the sciences. I taught Philosophy, you know.' I almost say yes, I do know, but of course that would give the game away, so I let him carry on. 'We worked in different parts of the campus.'

He puts two glasses and an ashtray on the table. It is half-full and looks like he had been rolling tobacco in newspaper. I distinctly see the logo of the Morning Message on one of the burnt scraps.

Score four.

'Oh, he had nothing but good words for you, Maxim Ostropovich. He often regaled us with tales of how you went up against the governors in defence of them all. He was quite proud to have known you. He even gave me one of your books.'

Oh yes, I think: we know you've written books. Maybe a long time ago, but what a man writes, so must he live.

Score five.

Maxim Ostropovich looks extremely pleased and starts pouring out the vodka. We get a few down us while we carry on exchanging pleasantries. I get out my cigarettes – proper, pre-rolled ones – and leave them on the table where we can both get at them. Maxim puts one out and lights another; I wave my hand. Carry on, I say: we rebels must stick together. For hours we talk and talk and more vodka goes down our throats. I make sure mine is still half-full when the refill comes – that way he gets twice as much down his neck as me – and we talk of old times and the college and my make-believe uncle, who actually was shot by mistake at a bread riot in the capital over ten years ago. I quote some of his own aphorisms from the book he published in his glory days at the University. It had only been printed on the University Press and we had a devil of a time getting our hands on a copy. And when we did, it was hardly worth it – fifty pages of sanctimonious drivel about the need to honour the individual and the inviolable rights of each man to speak his mind and live according to his own truth, blah blah blah.

Score six. This Maxim is very nearly our perfect profile for the Scribbler. All I need do now is find the pens and paper. That he has them, I have no doubt. I have already noticed the blue stains on his fingers. After an age of babbling, I manage to persuade him to sign my precious copy of his book. I check the handwriting while I'm having a piss, and score the top points. It looks pretty much the same as the Scribbler's, whose pathetic poems were all hand-written in untidy block capitals.

Quarter-way down the second bottle, I decide it's time to get off. I persuade Maxim to write a note to my uncle and he trots over to the desk and gets out pen and paper. Ha! I knew he would have it somewhere! I glimpse a fine big block of the white stuff and a whole carton of pens. I set a candle on the table. I lay out the utensils. I pour more vodka into his glass. I tell him I'll make coffee while he gets started. I go into the kitchen, put the water on the stove. I open the back door. All I have to do now is head down the street and alert the back-up crews. They'll send a professional along shortly and set a fire in the kitchen. The fire-crews will be too busy to get there in time, having been called out to a large conflagration on the city's edge, and the house will be destroyed; the owner along with it. He will be found slumped at the table with two large vodka bottles and the remains of pens and paper. I'll return to barracks and compare notes with the others. Us Visitors will recount our scores. Five and upwards brings the fires, and only if we're sure, and I couldn't have been surer. We'll wait a couple of days to check the Scribbler has gone for good, then we'll hold a party in the barracks. The Commander himself said he would attend.

Well, that was what should have happened. Instead, I'm lying in Maxim Ostropovich's garden, half in the radish patch, halfway up the steps. I'm still waiting for the bastard to come back but he's forgotten, and none of the neighbours seem to be in. At least the cold has killed some of the pain in my ankle but I've frozen in place on the step. Oddly, it seems as if someone has thrown a couple of buckets of water down them, so that there's a sort of slide where the water's frozen on its way down. I can't figure it out. I can hear Maxim doing something or other inside. It's getting very dark, and I'm sleepy. I must have nodded off.

Someone is tapping at my chest. Thank God! Help at last! I can't speak, but I try and raise a hand to say hurry up and get a move on, but my rescuer is already standing up. He's got a medical bag in one hand – at least I think it's a medical bag, and he's heading down the path. Why is he going away already? Is he going to get a stretcher? It's very cold. It's very dark.

Private Makar Makarovich was found the next day by his unit. The house was deserted when they broke the front door down, and Makar was still stuck to the steps, his arms out-flung, his eyes open and frosted. Someone had been through his pockets and his papers were missing. There was something pinned to his coat-front. A note:

> *From the mouse to the cat:*
> *I told you it sometimes happens.*
> *One day it will happen all the time.*
> *Until then, goodbye,*
> *And thanks for the drink.*

Private Makar Makarovich was buried with full military honours and promoted posthumously to Officer First Class. The Message told the extended story of his exciting capture of The Scribbler and how the traitor had managed to fire upon the Private with a secreted revolver when, in his compassion, the Private had turned his back for a moment to fetch the distressed prisoner a glass of water. His comrades had arrived too late to save the soldier: another brave man lost to the cause of upholding the People's Revolutionary Government.

The Scribbler, however, and The Morning Message was insistent on this point, had not got away, and had written his last poem.

As the old, old saying goes: you can't always believe everything you read.

As the Scribbler would have added: *let us read everything, and maybe we will try.*

The Damascene Cure

If you've ever skivvied on a ship you'll know what it is to ache until your bones feel sodden-drunk. Your bed is a plank of wood and your blanket a sack which stinks of scale-rubbings, and salt encrusts your eyes and mouth, scrapes your cheeks, stings your sores. You're force-fed fish and rotting biscuits at every meal, of which – thank God for small mercies – there aren't many. The pride I had was knocked from me like wind from a sail in the doldrums – it slips away without you knowing and then when you finally look, there's nothing left. And so there you stand in a pool of your own waste and sewage, nothing to push you on or pull you back. *Il Mare Marrone* the sailors call it; I call it *The Shit-Brown Sea.*

I began as Balbi Bartolommeo, and had ambitions to marry well. I had in my sights one Euphemia Jocastinnia Galeazzo di Medici, descendant of that famous Florentine family which vomits Popes and Dukes at every turn. She wasn't a beauty: thin as a pear-stalk, skin like flour. But her family had as many palaces as there are bridges in Venice, and I felt it was where I belonged. Accident bore me to poverty and hired me as a costermonger, but my eyes saw the good things in the world, and by God, I meant them to be mine.

'Eh Balbi, Balbi. Are you going to sleep all day? There's flies in the soup and the ladle's crusty as an orphan's nose. Balbi, eh Balbi!'

The elbow I have been using as a pillow is knocked from under me and my feet kicked off the stool.

'What's all the blasted hurry?' As usual I have been awoken from my dreams by my associate, Ludwig Vitruvius Scamozzi, who has all the brains of a bear and is not of dissimilar size. Mozzi stirs the soup with his usual grace.

'You're splashing it all over the floor,' I point out helpfully.

'It hasn't burned. I was watching it all the while.'

Mozzi spits from the corner of his mouth – a most impressive skill – and mutters something which sounds very like *Bah!* – an English expression he has picked up from the gaming den we favour for skinning the foreign fops. A pool of green scum lands in front of me, followed by a truncheon of yesterday's bread. Sighing at the paltry repast I turn my thoughts again to Euphemia and the future, but as I watch Mozzi cram himself into his chair and start to stir his soup with his thumb, I give up. As any good soldier knows, it is useless to fight when the battle is already done.

'So, Mozzi, what is our plan of the day?'

It is Sunday afternoon after all, and we have been released from the shackles of the shop. The till was kind enough to oblige me with several notes whilst the boss's back was turned, and wealth is of no use if it is not spent.

Mozzi mumbles through a slurp of soup. 'You can make your own plans, Balbi; I'm off with a girl.'

I knit my brows together so hard that for a moment I cannot see. It pains me that such a man as Ludwig Scamozzi can have girls after him as constant as a snail has a trail. They take him dancing or gondoliering or both, clutch continually at his brawny arms, and tuck their heads with sickening regularity below his enormous chin which, incidentally, might be a buttock for the size and depth of its cleft. I know all this because I have followed him on occasion, just to make sure he wasn't making the whole thing up. It is rather dispiriting when a man who can hardly do up his boots attracts women like ants to a picnic.

'Who is it today?' I feign an interest I do not feel. 'Maria from the hat shop?'

Mozzi slurps up the end of his soup, runs his tongue around the bowl.

'Maria? Hardly!' He wipes the crumbs from the thicket of hair which lines his unsavoury chin. 'Ancient history, friend. Three dates and she wanted me round to meet her dad. Not likely! says I, and scarpers. No dog collars for Mozzi, not yet at any rate.'

'How about coming down The Twisted Pipe? Few jugs of landlord's worst and a game of cards? Your pick?' It's a forlorn hope, but I try.

Mozzi puts the bowl on the floor for the cat to clean and pats his stomach.

'That's a good one! You think I'd give up *Angelina Forgazzi*,' he hisses the name across the table, 'so's I can get skinned at cards by you?'

I can hardly believe it! Angelina Forgazzi has a passably pretty face and enough money to bury an army in. I gasp, no doubt just as Mozzi intended.

'I'd ask you with me, but what with all that sleeping you've been doing, I expect you forgot you're to be at the docks to meet the Syrian ship for the boss's order. Quite a lot of exotica, I gather. Though not as exotic as Angelina.'

I'm still gaping when he jams his hat on his head with his customary lack of style, clinks his money purse and cheerily says good-bye.

Down at the docks a westerly wind began to blow, spattering my new silk sleeves with daubs of rain. I walked the several piers looking for the *Southern Siren*, slipping on fish scurry and dropping my gloves into a puddle of rotten bait-gut. There was no option but to abandon them, and wish them a long life being nibbled by lobsters and eels. I cursed myself for not bringing my cape as the squall rose to a shriek and started flinging hailstones around like a mad dice-man. How can a day start in summer and end in winter?

I almost missed the ship when I finally reached the third pier, clutching the brim of my hat with both hands. She was a scrub of a thing who had apparently been dragged through every marsh in Arab-land, judging by the sludgy green weeds festooning every anchor-chain and rope. The gangplank was awash with slime and algae – as now were my boots. No-one appeared to question my arrival; in fact no-one appeared at all. The deck was deserted, apart from a square mountain of boxes lashed to the gunwales and some rather intriguing caskets which were loose along the boards. Looking all the while over my shoulder, I tapped several with my toe-cap and was rewarded with several metallic clinks. Still no-one appeared. The rain was falling in spades by now, and the wind was whipping at every loose tarp and linen it could find. The docks stood deserted, inhabited only by the bulky outlines of unloaded stock and the occasional scurry of stevedores heading for the nearest inn. A heap of sail-sacks came flying across the deck and I grabbed one of them by the tail. With barely a thought, I stuffed the sack with two, three, four of the small boxes, slung it casually over my shoulder and legged it down the gangplank fast as I could. Slipping on the puddle-pocked cobbles it was all I could do to stay upright, and it was with a pang that I let go the rim of my hat to steady myself against the wall, watched it fly into the air like a blue jay, before plummeting into the filthy water between the *Southern Siren* and the *Arms of Sister Mary*. Still, the greater good of the laden sack felt solid and wet against my back.

My birthdays are no great shakes, primarily aimed at getting as drunk as possible as pleasantly as possible, depending on how much I have filched from the till when Armand, our boss, is not looking. Mozzi usually leaves me a little gift – a small wheel of cheese perhaps, or a new cravat; once even a pair of tickets for the theatre and a cheap girl thrown in for free. Thus I have little to compare to the thrill of lining up four caskets of unknown content upon the table in front of me. I have changed my clothes, dried my hair, put my boots by the fire which I have lit, and which is warming a pan of wine. The smell of cloves and allspice percolates through the smoke, sweetening the air. I have lit a pipe aiming to calm myself, but knock it out almost immediately. I cannot wait! The suspense is too great! My fingers tremble as I undo the buckles of the first casket imagining a scatter of loose diamonds in plush purple velvet, a score of gold rings set with amber, an Egyptian necklace of brightest blue scarabs, a dozen silver dice alight with rubies. I lift the lid slowly, poke my nose close and smell the leather scorched by desert sand, cracked by sea-salt, damp from our Mediterranean rain. Without warning, something shoots from the box and catches me in the corner of the eye. Shocked, I leave go of the lid which falls back up on its hinge and a ghastly rasping sound is heard. There is no word for the horror which pours through me like iced water and prickles upon my skin. Inside are three scorpions, small, the colour of sand. Two seemingly dead, the other most definitely not. Already the light is being expunged from my eye as the poison creeps from one side to the other, a curtain slowly dropped to drive the day into night.

I did not die that evening, nor the next. The pain was vast and I screamed and writhed, foam cascading from my mouth, my muscles cramped and locked. Armand laid a compress across my eyes and cursed me for a fool. He fired me on the spot and deducted his medical treatment from my final wage. My eye is black as a rotten walnut and the necrosis has stolen half my nose and cheek. The judge has given me a choice: sail with the *Siren* for as long as they'll have me for as little as they'll give me, or hang.

And so I am on the *Siren* now, looking across a grey, malevolent sea, watching the only place I have known disappear. Mozzi came to see me off, whispered in my ear as I leant forward to shake his hand:

'A man will get what he deserves. Whatever's in the box, he put it there.'

His glove is loose. It comes off in my hand. Mozzi smiles, wriggles his fingers, shows off the fine gold rings lined up on his knuckles, sparkling with opals and jade.

'You picked the wrong one!' He laughs and crams his hat upon his head. 'Enjoy the sea, Balbi. May your fortune find you.'

I clutch at the rails, curse the man who believed sand-scorpions would cure his pox, curse Mozzi for having the luck of the devil, curse myself for indolence and greed. Swear to pick the better box next chance comes along.

The First Mate snarls some Arabic insult, so I turn my back on him and the world and head down to the galley to make the crew their soup. I suppose it is a trade of sorts, making soup. And it is the one time I thank God that the devil stole my nose.

The Rake-Maker's Garden

Pitch-pine for the shaft six foot long, ash for head and hoop, hammer in the sixteen teeth from silver birch and there you have your hay rake. And my father has a garden full of trees. Only small, copse-height, limbs lopped. At night they sigh like the amputees they are and bow their heads below the moon. In the noise and rage of the autumn storms they wail their discontent to the wind, fling decomposing body-parts to the ground in angry despair.

My father gets ill on the Sunday after we've come back from church. The Minister was at Ezekiel, telling us about salting babies, purging them of devils and sin. We make our way home along the lanes, father shouting about how useless Ministers were the world over.

'Wedding and deading is all they're good for. Salt indeed! Been using it for years without his say-so. Stops the slugs and snails eating new growth. Keeps the deer from stripping the bark from the trees. You'll need to learn it, boy, and not from him, when we finally get you married off to that Tyndall girl. By Christ, she's taking some time to grow! Still, I was speaking to Coxie only yesterday, and he's agreed on next year. We've settled that I'll plant up the West Field with more trees, build a second work-shed on site for you and the girl.'

He digs me in the kidneys with his stick. 'Nice and cosy for the newly-weds and if you work hard, which by God I'll make sure you do, we'll soon be employing lads from the village to help out. Have a bonny little industry going. Think of the money, boy, and the Tyndall girl is fairly fine and growing in all the right places, and I'm sure mother wouldn't mind me saying so.'

He winks at mother and slaps me across the head with his hat. Tiny scribbles of rake-wood get caught in my hair and a sprinkle of sawdust makes my eyes swim.

We arrive home and take off our best clothes, drink tea, eat seed-cake and sugar-dumplings. By six o'clock, father has swollen up like a radish in water. We have to take all his clothes off before buttons fly and the belt-buckle breaks. We can't get him up the stairs and he won't shut up moaning, so we lay him on the table between blanket and eiderdown. I think we left a dumpling under there. He's fair bursting with sweat and his veins rise purple, the skin straining and stretching to keep his insides in. By Tuesday morning he is dead, and not a day too soon. He's been shouting the house down, stinking out every corner. We've had the windows open fit to freeze us and the place still smells. We get his coffin out of the work-shed and try to squash him in, but the timbers start to split before we've got him halfway. So we wrap him up in a three-sheet shroud, let the Minister do his mouthing, then lower him down quick as we can because the weight is making our elbows crack, and cover him over before he pops.

By Friday I have cleared a space amongst the pines and chopped them up into stacks. Mother stands at the kitchen sink and weeps into the dishwater, her hands turning into prunes, her face the colour of bacon.

'Why oh why?' is all she can say whenever I go in, so I stay outside and sleep in the work-shed. I have burned all the half-made rakes, snapped their staves, slashed their grinning hoops, broken their teeth.

By summer I have cleared a small glade of land, torn out every stubborn stump, dug up every clinging root. The soil has sunk and found a level; I have bulked it up with sawdust and chips of wood (I have plenty) and covered it over with fermented dung and rotting leaves.

Mother still weeps at the window. I still sleep in the shed. It is cleared of wooden limbs and boiling-pots and buckets of nails. It is a nursery now of plants and cuttings and shrubs and flowers and bulbs.

In spring I put in my garden a statue, a circular flowerbed her skirt. This I divide into four and further pleat each section into three. Every month shall have its chance and I plant as it will grow, a revolution slow and sure, a wave riding the movement of the earth. In January I have winter honeysuckle, eye-bright and fragrant; in February I have drops of snow amongst the white and yellow aconite; in March I have double-headed daffodils and primrose smiling at the watery sun; tulips burst their bulbs in April and stand as goblets for the dew.

My statue, a slender gnomon, tells me what is the time of day; my flowers whisper the season, speak to me the month. I gather the seeds and guard the fruit. Each year my wheel will get a little bigger as I move the border back, advancing further into the trees. The shadow of my statue will stretch her hand forth over the years. My work-shed will smell of new-sprung shoots and layering leaves. I have planted currants and figs, apples and raspberries. I have made a hedge out of box and bay, coaxed ivy up the hard bare walls.

My mother still weeps so I bake her a cake for her birthday. She takes longer than father but doesn't swell up hardly at all and dies the following week. I put her in my father's coffin, the one we couldn't use, open his grave to drop her in. When we scrape up the earth we find he has quite disappeared, leaving only a scrap of ragged sheet and the gnarl of some green-mouldered bones.

I move back into the house and do not marry Mary Tyndall. The next year, I have roses climbing over the windows and hollyhocks singing to me in the sun. I keep one rake to scrape the leaves in autumn, and fill the shed with apples and pears. The hideous lop-limbed trees which darkened my youth are gone. The wretched reek of knacker's glue will never be smelt again. Dad and Mam at last have left me on my own. Winter comes and I sit by the fire and smoke, play cards, drink plum shrub and burdock beer, pat the collie bitch who lies on my feet.

Every spring I chop down more of the past, axe it into logs, make chairs and stools to sell at market, build the woodpile higher.

Every year the garden grows and the light stretches farther into the wood-meadows.

Every night I set a spill to the fire, turn my back to the grate, feel the last warmth of the sun through the window, watch its flame bleed from the hills.

Every morning sees me and my tea and a stroll with dawn down the garden.

Under the Ybb, and Over

Leaning against the wall of Lorenz Grillinger's shed were three lutes made of tortoise shells of increasing size. He'd found heaps of the dead animals when, for the first time ever, he'd gone up on his roof. He lived in Winkelmüthe-am-Ybbs and his house backed onto the dockyard by the river. Three years it had taken him to convert the big wool-barn into somewhere habitable, grubbing meantime at the factory to make the money he needed. Cleaning out dies was his job, and he hated it. But at last his wool-barn was looking good: he'd strengthened the walls and put in a clerestory, its windows facing to the east. From here, he was on a direct line of sight with the clock tower of the monastery on the other side of the river – the one which had its hands fixed at ten to nine, which was the hour when the Kuruz invaders had swept down from the hills and driven the people through the town like cattle, forced them onto the frozen river where they fell through the ice and drowned in the undercurrent, blue lips and hands scrabbling at the belly of the Ybb. Some survived by skittering lightly across the surface to reach the other side, or spread-eagling themselves until the monks could haul them in with ropes and hooks tied to long branches. Mostly they just died where they lay, killed by the cold and the night and the fear which froze the sweat on their faces into fetters, binding them irrevocably to the ice.

That was a hundred years ago now, but the wind still sighed below the bridge when the storms began to gather, and carved strange shapes across the snow on the banks and made the mists rise like wraiths from the hard winter-white of the water.

When Grillinger was a boy, he'd sit on the springy mounds of moss which grew green alongside the Ybb, and cut reeds to make whistles and blow hemlock stems into pipes, make fennel stalks into boxes. He'd known they were listening, those lost ancestors, felt their cold, old breath on his hair, watched the thistledown waft around them as it blew across the meadows; hoped he was comforting them a little with his tunes.

There had been an odd occurrence in Winkelmüthe the year before, which had led to Grillinger's discovery on his roof. It had been the last day of March when the small vessel had been sighted far down river, its mast tall as teasel on the horizon, its sail the pale mauve of an opium poppy. Grillinger was probably the first one to have seen the small boat bobbing its way up the waters of the Ybb, still slush and slow at the banks where the snow still came down from the hills, and the ice still cracked against the mud. He shaded his eyes from the rising sun which cast everything in a copper glow, burnished the water with bronze. The barque was oddly shaped – he could see that from here: the front rose up like a swan, the stern swooped down to a shallow bow. He watched it a few moments, then turned back to his work.

He was busy splitting glass into rings. Every other evening he trundled a little cart around the three ale-houses of the town and collected the bottles he found broken-necked on the pavements before them and in the courtyards behind. He wore thick mittens made from sacking. He'd learned from the early, bare-handed days about the tiny glass-shards that got into his skin and later itched worse than scabie-mites, and that's some itching.

Back home he set his bottles on the large table he had built of elm and tiled over, put several pokers to heat on the fire. He filled each bottle with cheap oil drained from the barrels of pilchards he purchased every quarter from the dockyard. It was an elegant trick, to plunge a burning poker into the oil and split the glass neatly when the heat hit its rim. Carefully done, you got smooth-edged beakers or rings of glass to any width you pleased. He wired the rings into mobiles, sold them as bangles and napkin holders, fashioned them into tubes for wind-chimes. Every tree and bush in his own garden was hung with his rings, glistening like gossamer in the sun, spinning gently in the wind, sending out a hum that pervaded every corner of the garden, gave you the sensation of someone singing softly just out of reach.

He stopped working when he heard the bell of the factory toll. He leaned the pokers against the fire-dog, wiped the tiles down with a cloth, stood as he always did in the doorway, wishing he could stay. Then he closed the door, pulled the bolt, hove the hasp of the padlock into place.

He was jealous of his secrets, as most men are.

Grillinger had done his shift, washed and wrung out his sweat-drenched clothes and hung them on the line; had warmed his plate of bean-and-pilchard stew. He could hear a hubbub somewhere out on the docks. He climbed the stairs, opened the door to his workroom and looked down upon the little crab-like pier which clung to the edge of the Ybb. He realised the strange boat must have tied up downstream and waited out the day so that, by evening, the townspeople would be falling over themselves with curiosity. A showman, thought Grillinger, and was about to turn away when he looked again. The stranger was just pulling in to the pier; he threw the rope to the gathering crowd, lowered the sail; he began pulling a tarpaulin off a great chest with metalled corners shining like silver. Something flashed beneath the bows of the boat, underneath the pier. If Grillinger hadn't known better, he'd have sworn it to be a pair of porpoise. He shook his head and turned away, stoked the fire, added the pokers, set a few bottles on his table. He was in the middle of gently pouring in the oil, careful not to cause a drip or make the level sway and ruin the circle, when there came a loud battering on his downstairs door. He stopped mid-pour, his elbow cocked, his fingers tight around the flask. Someone was calling his name. Annoyed, he replaced the flask on its shelf, rolled down his sleeves, and went down the stairs. Outside, there was a milling of people all holding up a couple of coins and shouting for bottles and jars. Grillinger took a step backwards, held up his arm in front of his face. He didn't like to see so many people all in one place, hardly ever spoke unless he had too. The noise was unbearable. Then Erich Haffhölzer, the foreman at the factory, emerged and told everyone to go away and wait at the Town Hall. He knew everybody's face and name and could fire whomever he wanted, so despite the gruff murmur of discontent, off everyone went, clinking their coins back inside their purses.

Haffhölzer brought in the only man left, the boatman; led him into Grillinger's house as if it had been his own.

'I want this man to show you something, die-cleaner,' said Haffhölzer, addressing Grillinger by his factory name, giving him his orders, telling him his place. The boatman smiled; his teeth were crooked, his skin was dark. He dragged a casket in from the street. It wasn't the chest, it was something smaller. The moon was climbing above the monastery and shone down through the open doorway. The boatman produced a glass jar, shook it, lifted off the lid, held up a finger while he placed the jar on the open lid of the casket, let the liquid settle. He took out several vials and shook a few grains from each into the beaker.

'Watch!' Haffhölzer whispered, and Grillinger watched. At first there was nothing. Then he leaned closer: saw tiny towers begin to rise within the glass, minarets and gardens appearing in blues and greens and pomegranate pinks.

'It is magic!' said Haffhölzer, his eyes fixed on the glass.

'It is chemistry,' said the boatman, and shook his little vials of sulphates and salts.

Grillinger took the boatman up through his workroom to the short metal stair-case leading to the roof. They took up a table and lit it all around with candles and lamps; they gathered every beaker and jar they could carry and filled each one with the secret ingredients, watched as they grew in their underwater pools, fountains of colour, miniature towns, beds of exotic flowers. The townsfolk came up the steps one by one, paid their money, sat for several hours as landscapes and architectures precipitated stone by stone, flower by flower. The only annoyance was the smell of decay and rotting flesh. And that came from the piles of tortoises heaped at one end of the roof. The boatman, who had grown innumerable miracles in innumerable towns, went off to investigate. Grillinger saw him go, watched him kick softly at the untidy pile, heard a clatter of half-emptied shells as they slipped like scree. It had puzzled him when he'd first moved into his barn how every now and then, when he was hanging out his work-clothes to dry, he had seen the smashed carapaces of small tortoises littering the yard.

He'd got hit on the head once and had gazed upwards into a clear blue sky and wondered.

Now he knew.

The tortoises had been tipped into a heap from the several smashed crates which lay cock-angled beside the boatman. Some were still caught between the palings of the boxes, a few desiccated heads and feet, bits of shell cracked open by the gulls. But mostly they had been crushed and suffocated by their fellows where they lay. A few had managed to crawl out and thrown themselves off the precipice of the roof. Some had taken the other direction but had died of starvation and cold. Grillinger had thought of his ancestors freezing and heaped under and over the ice of the Ybb. He shivered. Heard people moving, starting to get up to leave, the boatman turning his back on the turtles-heaps, carefully tipping the water back into his flask, selling the miracle jars to the spectators for souvenirs.

They'd all had their share that night: Haffhölzer, the boatman and Grillinger, but mostly what Grillinger remembered was the steady crunch of shells breaking underfoot as his neighbours and work-mates criss-crossed the roof and made their way back down the stairs. He'd looked across the river, seen the hands of the monastery clock still stuck at ten to nine as they always had been. As they always should be. Wondered whether the better death was separation from the earth beneath the icy waters of the Ybb, or asphyxiation by one's peers on some isolated island roof. Thought probably he'd prefer to die alone. Would probably choose the water, if anyone ever asked.

But for now, Grillinger would make his wind-chimes out of rings of glass and set his lutes to make the empty tortoise shells sing. He thought of them piled up there on his roof waiting to be turned into lute-bowls. He wondered if they had been meant for soup or plates or pets; whether someone had been supposed to collect them. Realised how versatile those tortoises could be. Thought of Erich Haffhölzer when he'd come back later that night, a few too many drinks inside his skin, crashed his way unasked into Grillinger's home, found the die-cleaner still tidying up his roof. How the foreman had demanded a bigger share of the money. Threatened Grillinger's job at the factory. How he'd slipped on a tortoise in the dark and gone headlong over the parapet and into the dockyard below.

At least that's what he'd told everybody, and that's what they had believed. No-one had liked Erich Haffhölzer, especially not once he'd made foreman.

That Erich had got far too big for his boots.

Grillinger often thought about that boatman and the tumble of turtles upon his roof. Occasionally he wondered about the boatman's boat, and the porpoises, but what with the fuss over Erich Haffhölzer, the boatman had set sail and gone before he'd had time to ask. He doubted the boatman would ever come back. Some men are only made for going forward. Grillinger didn't mind. He was content. He had secrets of his own, and knew there were things a man should never tell, even if he could.

The Insanity of Sheep

Professor Jorge Häagen came into the lecture theatre ten minutes late. He gave this talk once a semester, and once a semester he was late. He brought no notes or papers. He had no briefcase. He went straight to the lectern, turned his back to his audience and chalked a word on the board. The chalk broke in two and fell to the floor, bouncing shortly on the wooden planks, a faint cloud of dust gathering in the turn-ups of his trousers.

'Frenzical, from Greek *phrenitis*, an inflammation of the mind. A burning from the inside, a fire which seeks release in a violent act.'

He poured some water from the carafe on the desk into his glass. Once a semester, and once a semester only, he had replaced half the water with gin. He took a long draught then ran his gaze over the rows of faces staring down at him. They might have been watermelons for all he cared.

'The exemplar of the frenzical is found with frequency in the fanatic, from the Latin *fanaticus*, "belonging to the temple:" one who believes himself inspired by the breath of his gods.'

He steadied his hands, and wrote the words on the board.

'And there have been tens of thousands of gods throughout human culture, and when one set of people with one set of gods confront another set of people with a different set of gods, you get conflict. And when people believe they are inspired by their gods, that they love their gods and their gods love them, there is only one result. And that is chaos.'

The Professor blinked behind his glasses and glanced around the room. He saw the bowed heads, heard the scritch of pencils scribbling across paper. The Professor tightened his fingers around the stump of broken chalk and closed his eyes. And it happened all over again.

I had come to the Caucasus, to Azerbaijan. I had sailed from Denmark to Istanbul, crossed the Black Sea, trudged the mountain trails by mule. My aim: to study a language spoken by the single village of Ruch Archi in Western Dagestan. By now, it is most likely extinct, and I will have outlived a language.

You may have guessed that I never reached that village. My guide deserted after knocking me over the head with a rock. He stole everything bar my boots, whose laces his arthritic fingers could not untie, and my trousers, which he could not remove over my boots. He left my notebooks, scattered about me blank-faced where they fell, spines broken, ink blurring in the mist that had dropped down from the hills.

I awoke to find a man poking at my feet with the rusting barrel of his gun. When he saw my eyelids open, the man increased his prodding until at last I sat up despite the abominable pain in my head and the feeling I was about to be sick.

'What are you doing here?' he asked. He was speaking Udi, or something very like it, and I had enough of that language to be able to mumble a sparse reply. Whether he believed me or not, I cannot say. He took a water-skin from the saddlebag of his mule and flung it at me, along with a moth-eaten blanket which smelled badly of sweat. I counted the fleas as they jumped from the seams, and thanked God for my rescuer. His face was hidden by a large dark beard and a straggle of long hair. He stared at me a moment, his brown eyes bloodshot and narrowed against the sun, and then he slung his gun about his back and called for me to follow. I managed to grab several of my notebooks as I stumbled off behind him, my mind already calculating the phonemes of his dialect, my fingers itching to jot them all down. We appeared to be headed straight up the rock face, but on looking harder, I could see a path vaguely outlined by a spill of stones, and at top, the kohl-black eyes of the caves.

'Why do you hold your mouth open like that?' It was my rescuer, at present peeling the skin off a lizard and offering me a chunk which had been blackened on the fire. He had brought me to a large cave, the entrance hidden by a scrub of acacia, guarded by scrawny men clutching rifles, ancient bandoliers across their chests. There was no surprise at my arrival, and I supposed they'd seen us coming up the hill. Still, the lack of curiosity seemed odd, the few raised eyebrows seeming hardly sufficient for the event, but then who was I to judge another race?

They watched as I parked my blanket on a rock, then ignored me, gathering in a squat around the fire. The men – who numbered twenty-three, not counting the outside guards – forgot me as they ate a meal of skink and goat, drank fermented milk, sang songs and talked. From this I gathered something of who they were, matched their tales with the stories and histories I had read.

They were of an ancient warrior line called The Turkomen of the Black Sheep who had once ruled all Armenia and Azerbaijan – hence their use of Udi, a language attached to the Armenian Church for over a thousand years. The Black Sheep had been massacred by the White Sheep who had been massacred in turn by the Persians. Such was a common theme in every country's history, but here, in these hills, something of the Black Sheep had survived their past. They had lived in bitter isolation, words and beliefs becoming peculiar to themselves. They had become a race apart, their hatred for their enemies distilled, all vapidity vanishing like water boiling from a bowl. I felt excitement at my discovery: there was so much to find out – their social rules, their idiom and song, the eccentricities of their religion and tongue. These people lived for their Armenian God, whom they believed most grievously wronged. They hid in these hills, and struck like a snake from behind a rock, biting their enemies quick and hard then withdrawing without hardly being seen. The papers I would write when I got home! My name would gain such notoriety! The journals and newspapers would come running with outrageous offers of money and coverage! At the very least, I would be offered a permanent position at the university. Eagerly I sharpened my pencil against the rock as best I could and turned my ears to their words as they crabbed around the fire. Delight disappeared as I listened and the night wore on. Far from the fame and fortune I had imagined, it turned out that my options were horrifyingly few.

'He's not from here,' argued one, his scuffed boots kicking roasted figs from the fire. 'Why should we care? We should do what our fathers would have done and leave him as an example to others.'

'The trees aren't big enough around here,' responded another, 'and besides, it would be a waste of nails.'

'And who would come looking anyway?' offered his neighbour, leaving off sucking his marrow-bone for a moment to consider the old idea of crucifixion. 'He's a foreigner, and worse, he's a teacher. Thinks he can tell us things or study us like the locusts they look at down on the plain – they pull their legs off one by one and pin them to bits of glass. I know, I've seen them that time I was spying out the new, so-called mosque. Maybe we should do it to him before he does it to us.'

'We could tie him to a board and roll him down the cliff,' this one had a glint of gold amongst his blackened teeth, 'teach the teacher how it goes around here when you stick your nose in.'

'And break all his bones at the same time,' countered my rescuer, 'and what would be the use of him then?'

'What's the use of him now?' asked several at the same time, laughing at their wit.

'Oh, I can think of something,' said the man, ripping a strip of skin from his skink. 'Trees don't grow plums for nothing. When God gives you a gift, He doesn't mean for you to sit on your backside and watch it rot.'

His companions fell quiet. I heard the crackle of the fire and my heart thumping hard against my ribs, felt the blanket crawl around my shoulders, sharp rocks against my back, the void waiting to empty me of my soul as a broken ewer seeps water, forever useless, into the sand.

'It's a reasonable choice.' He was spelling the thing out for me a second time. 'After all, we are not barbarians, and a man is a man no matter his tribe and must do his duty to his people and his God. I will ask you again...'

I started to laugh, the situation seemed so absurd, but he

just watched me, his knife raised, glinting in the flames.

'Again I ask,' he repeated, 'you understand me?'

'Yes! No!' It appeared to me that I shouted, but amongst these men who were hard and dark as the walls of our confining cave, I might have been a wasp in a bottle for all the noise I made. The choice seemed impossible, and yet of course I knew it had already been made. That I had made it. My only consolation was knowing that most men would have chosen the same. My rescuer looked pleased. Despite my pathetic protests, he knew what was in my eyes. He came over to where I sat huddled at the back of the cave. He gave me a cup of beer and watched until I had drained it to the rancid dregs. He spoke to the others but his eyes never left my face.

'It is a simple matter.' No mouth was visible under that gleaming beard and he stood as a totem before me. 'You will deliver our message and we will let you live. We are fair men and we will even let you choose: left or right?'

My legs wobbled as I approached the old Armenian church. The saints which had adorned its face had been hacked from the rock and lay scattered and broken around my feet. The walls had been white-washed, the murals obliterated, the pews were turned to the wall. The altar had been stripped of its cloth, the monstrance and chalice thrown in contempt to the bare mud floor. The men on their prayer-mats turned in annoyance as I clattered my way through the door. I did not remove my boots. I had not removed them since the day my guide deserted and left me for dead.

The men watched in horror as the dishevelled form stumbled past them. They made no move to stop him or to clutch at the dirty blanket hanging from his shoulders which was apparently held up by dried mud and blood. The Imam appeared from what had been the sacristy and came forward, holding his arms wide apart, ready to stop the stranger but fearing for his touch. An awful noise came from the stranger's throat as he repeated several words over and over, and only when he stood directly before the Imam could he make out the words.

'If your right hand offends thee, cut it off; if your right hand offends thee, cut it off; if your right hand...'

His accent was strange, his face European; he stank like a mongrel, he looked as if he had never slept, his arm was strapped to his waist by a dirty bandage, he had a small barrel around his neck. With some difficulty the stranger unslung the barrel and held it out with his free hand, put it on the stone of the altar where it fell to its side and rolled off the edge. It hit the floor with a hollow thud, and the old wood slats splintered and broke. A deal of liquid slopped into the red sand and, as the rotting wooden ribs fell away, there lay Jorge's hand. The sight of it lying upturned in front of him, separate from him, away from him, was too much. He fell onto his remaining hand and knees, retching so badly his lungs almost turned themselves inside out.

Professor Jorge Häagen finished writing and went to put the chalk in the chalk-rest by the board. He missed, and it fell amongst the dusty scatter already lying on the floor. His clumsiness evoked a slight undertow of laughter, whispers about the Professor being drunk, watching him sway slightly, his hands in his pockets, his glasses atypically askew. The students coughed in the small silence, then started to pack away their books and pencils, fold glasses into cases, chatter amongst themselves.

The Professor went back to the desk and drained his glass, watched as the students pushed and jostled, laughed a noisy way out the back of the auditorium. He left the dais, switched out the lights, stood there in the dark. He heard the sound of the man sharpening his axe, he felt the cracked leather strap that tied him to the rock, he heard the whistle as the blade severed the air in two, he felt the awful shock of being parted from himself. He looked and saw his hand sliced clean through at the wrist, saw his fingers twitch, the hot blood pouring, the sting of the alcohol as someone shoved his stump into a barrel of corn-brew. Lucky for him he was unconscious when they stretched his skin and blanket-stitched the flaps together over the severed bone.

He'd been right about the journalists who'd flocked from all over the world to talk to him, but it was not for his groundbreaking linguistic breakthroughs or his discovery of an ancient bloodline thought extinct. The militia went storming up to the caves to catch the desecrators of the mosque but they had long gone, leaving only a blackened fire and a pile of skink bones. They did find Jorge's satchel and his notebooks, but all the pages had been eaten out by mice; the leather leaned against the rock, its front flapped open by its feet. Ants had eaten the stitching from the holes, left the satchel with the page-less books and the broken sticks of graphite denuded of their wood. The militia had stamped down from the mountain and swore they would track the villains down to the ends of the earth, but within a month the excitement died down and they forgot their promise.

Jorge's hand was forever gone from him but not forever gone. Doctor Padresh Hossain had been called to the mosque which was once an Armenian church. He'd been asked to identify the hand as human and the human as handless, in case the whole episode was a hoax. He'd examined the stranger and replaced the stitching of his stump, tried to distance the patient from his own delirium. When finally the stranger was carted off to the hospital, the doctor had asked the man if he wanted his hand to take with him. There was a certain worry about resurrection in some religions, he knew: about the body being in disparate bits. Apparently the man did not agree and only became hysterical when presented with the glass jar.

It sits now on the doctor's shelf, and he brings it out every now and then and tells the tale, though most of his visitors have heard it before. They always find it funny until the doctor makes them cup their hands around the jar and they see the awful loneliness of that hand and realise the manner of its parting. He gives them brandy, for he is no religious, and always raises a slight salute to the foreigner who came and went so alarmingly from their midst. Feels pity for him, and the slight tremor of fear to know that such things still existed, and not so far away that it might not have happened to any one of his neighbours or friends, or God forbid, to himself. Wonders what became of the rest of the wandering professor that did not sit upon his shelf in its jar.

Jorge is still sitting in the darkened room. The hands that are left him are on the table before him, one of them around a glass, the other unclipped and lying on its beetle-back, fingers curled towards the unlit moon of bulb, a shadow on a darkened cairn of books. Jorge has long passed weeping and cursing, and the anger has seeped out of him like blood in water, and over the years has been lost. He thanks God for gin, but before he has poured out the final finger, his head sinks to his arms and at last he allows himself to sleep – hopes, in the brief moment before he closes his eyes, that the world will somehow heal itself, let the lice fall from the seams of its blanket and stamp the last of them beneath its feet.

Hunting Ghosts

Emellan was woken by his own cry of shock and pain. His hands brushed ineffectually at the air as he tried to dislodge Borzac, whom he imagined to be lying across his chest. The wolfhound enjoyed demonstrating his loyalty by draping his weight across his master. Yet there was Borzac, snoring on the rug in front of the last glowing coals of the fire. Despite the warmth of the summer night, Emellan's hands and arms felt cold, and the tightness of his chest made it hard for him to breathe. He forced himself to sit up; counted his breaths slow and even up to ten. He should not have been alarmed, he should have been elated. This was why he had come. He was about to test his theory. Borzac lifted one ear and belly-crawled across the floor; he settled himself on Emellan's feet and gave him comfort. Emellan rested his hand over his heart. The pain was easing, the chill lifting like a morning mist. He smiled, drank the cold coffee on the bedside table, and glanced over to the window, seeking the dawn.

'You are saying there is no such thing as a soul!'

It was not a question, it was a shout of outrage, loudly endorsed by the crowd. Professor Emellan Richter of Mainz Academy held up his hands to hush the anger that rose against him. He had to raise his voice to be heard. He would be quite hoarse in the morning.

'My dear colleagues, students, please. I am not saying that at all. I am trying to explain certain phenomena in physical terms.'

'You would deny a spiritual dimension to our lives! You would rob us of our humanity! Would you have us crawl on our hands and knees instead of standing upright as God has decreed?'

It was Johann Dimiter, Divinity Don, devout Lutheran, a man who burned portraits of the pope publicly in the square, which hobby left the flagstones pocked and scorched.

Emellan flapped his hands, exasperated. He had known there would be opposition, but not this ridiculous theological charade.

'Gentlemen, please, please!'

He was shouting with the rest now, feeling ashamed to be taking part in what was descending to a cockfight.

'I am merely expressing an opinion! It is my belief that this rash of ghost-sightings is no more a Sign of Divine Intervention than if a flea leaped off a dog!'

At the sound of his generic name, Borzac, until now asleep under the large lectern, yawned massively and slowly got to his feet. He blinked at the noise, accustomed to his master's lectures, and lazily scanned the hall, vaguely hoping to sight a rabbit scut, or possibly a hare. The rotten egg caught him square on the nose, which on Borzac was large and sensitive. The smell he didn't mind, nor the small shards of shell pricking his skin. It was the surprise of the attack that made him skitter backwards, hitting the lectern at its weakest point, sending it crashing across the dais and into the desk, which collapsed spectacularly in a cloud of dust and paper. For a few moments the auditorium was silent, bar the echo of splintered wood meandering from wall to wall. Then Dimiter leapt upon the stage, kicking aside the debris, shouting of hubris and damnation.

'Could there be anything more clear than what has just happened? Has the Lord not shown His wrath?'

The crowd exploded. Chairs were knocked over, feet stamped, cries of 'Hurrah hurrah!' were heard.

Emellan sighed under Dimiter's gaze and bent to retrieve his scattered papers.

'Be warned,' hissed Dimiter into Emellan's stooped ear. 'God knows all and His Vengeance He will have.'

'I hope you told him to go hang himself!' exclaimed Hebbel as he consoled Emellan over a bottle of hock and a plate of pigs' trotters. Emellan said nothing and continued to spin an onion ring round his finger like a hoop.

'For God's sake, man, eat it, don't play with it! You knew this was going to happen. You know how stuffy all those old academics are.'

Emellan dropped the onion ring and took a large gulp of wine.

'You're right as always.' He spoke dully and with a heavy sigh. Hebbel banged the table with his fist, making the landlord glance over, momentarily arrested in the act of cleaning a grubby glass with a grubbier cloth.

'You're like an old woman! Chat, chat, moan, moan. Why don't you just do something about it? You think these ghost encounters are electromagnetic whatsits, then get down to Arnheiner and prove it.'

Hebbel drained his glass and stood to leave, patting the crumbs from his paunch.

'You believe in your damned theories? Then take a wager: one hundred krone that you can prove Dimiter wrong. One hundred! That should be enough to make a pauper like you finally get off his arse.'

So here was Emellan, sitting on the side of his bed with Borzac a giant slipper over his feet. He needed to get out there and check his instruments. He needed to see the graphite scribbles across his seismograph sheets, needed to check for the tiny tremors which threw out the density of electromagnetic waves needed to mimic the ghostly apparitions: the feeling of a tight weight upon one's chest, the coldness of the limbs, the hearing of a whine or moan within one's ears. Carefully he withdrew his feet from Borzac, who yawned, then retreated into a giant dormouse ball. He found his slippers and trod carefully across the carpet to the window, wrapped the quilt around his shoulders and gazed out to where the grass seemed grey and the trees scooped their backs over a river of ink. A faint breath of mist rose from the water, a swan shone white in its nest, several bats wove a way through the branches, swooped the surface, caught up moths tired from a night of nectar, flies that were beginning to wake. From nowhere, a large form appeared at the window, batted against the glass, wailed as if in pain. The hawkmoth was the size of a saucer, its death's head blurred on its back, the stripes on its body like prison bars. Once, twice, it dinted itself against the glass, before heading back into the dawn looking for a beehive to invade, rest in and rob. The sun was a golden thread around the hill-head and the sky glowed pink as dying coals.

Emellan turned away, intending to dress himself, when a movement caught his eye. He saw a dark form creeping across the grass, avoiding the gravel footpath. It was a man pulled into himself, plainly trying not to be seen, glancing around, checking for observers and spies. He took a direct line from the hotel lobby to the fishing pier. Once there, he went down on one knee, extracted something from his pocket. Emellan watched from his window as the man straightened, moved away, headed for the oak copse by the walled garden. Emellan's shock of realisation was so great he actually leapt to his feet and began for the door, tripping over the quilt which luckily broke his fall. He fought his way from it, losing his slippers, and grabbed his coat from the door. He ran down the stairs, not caring of the noise, and wrenched at the door, fumbling to turn the large iron key; he ran barefoot across the dew-drenched lawn and reached the orchard, panting, out of breath. There was the man, as Emellan knew he would be, approaching from the riverbank. From the pier to the copse to the orchard – exactly where Emellan had sited his recording instruments. He had a sharp pain in his side and bunched his fist into the stitch, tried to breathe calmly, counting from one to ten. But here he came, the saboteur, holding a hammer in his hand.

'AHA!' yelled Emellan triumphantly, leaping from the shadow of an old gnarled pear. Several fruits squashed under his feet like worms. Shocked, the man turned and the first rays of the sun rose from the hill and ripped the veil from his face. For a second or two the adversaries faced each other, standing barely two yards apart, the one in an undone coat, his feet slippered in rotten pears; the other with his face clarted with boot-polish, the hammer shining in his hands. Then the man was running like the devil across the lawn towards the house and Emellan was racing after him, slipping and sliding, losing his footing, eventually thumping to the ground onto a croquet hoop which groaned and bent under his weight. Hearing Emellan's cries of pain the other man hesitated, stopped and turned. He went back to his pursuer, hammer in hand. Emellan moaned and tried to get to his feet. His foe towered black above him, then he dropped the hammer, put his hands round Emellan's arm and pulled his friend to his feet.

'For God's sake,' muttered Emellan to Hebbel. 'Why?'

They sat in the breakfast room, although it was a full two hours before breakfast. The housemaid had been kind enough to bring them coffee and toast and a bowl of hot water for Emellan's feet. The seeds of mustard and anise dimpled around his ankles which had turned a rather alarming shade of blue. The water rippled as he clenched and unclenched his toes. Hebbel offered him a slug of some obnoxious brew he kept secreted in his flask. Emellan buried his face in a large handkerchief. The smell of camphor forced its way into his lungs, slow and certain as the stench of betrayal.

'I suppose it was a woman,' he eventually managed to croak. He was right: his voice had gone hoarse.

Hebbel's throat reddened but he slowly shook his head.

'I am afraid it is more sordid. It was money, old friend, merely money.'

And Hebbel explained that this very hotel was owned by his aunt and uncle, as he had mentioned, at the time that the Ghost Plague of Arnheiner had hit the headlines. Business had been bad before then, and suddenly their profits rose by five hundred percent, as did the allowance which they so kindly provided for him, so that he might continue to lead the light of science through these ignorant times.

'And indeed,' he added to soften the blow, 'I would have given you the hundred krone whichever way the bet went.'

'But you made sure I would lose!' growled Emellan.

Hebbel spread his hands out in front of him. 'Could I let you take away the livelihood of my only living relatives? Let them go back to hard times? Let the whole village go back to hard times?'

Emellan grunted. He saw the point even though he didn't like it.

'Why didn't you just tell me? Why did you have to smash my instruments? You know it has taken me five years – *five years!* – to amass the components. Five hard years, Hebbel.'

Hebbel gazed glumly at his hands.

'You still have the prototype,' he offered. Emellan snorted into his kerchief.

'You have destroyed my life's work for what? For a couple of years of prosperity?'

Hebbel slowly raised his eyes, looked closely at his friend.

'What do you mean? A couple of years? Surely this will be a permanent state of affairs?'

Another snort from Emellan that could most likely be interpreted as a laugh.

'Ha! Did you not think it strange that these phenomena came on so suddenly? In such a localised setting? No. Probably you did not. But I study these things, and I can tell you that these micro-seismic events are temporary. The activity is creeping up the tectonic crack away from the mountains, towards the plains. There are several more spots where it will localise before the energy of this slight tectonic shift disappears for another millennium into the Black Sea.'

There was silence for a few moments and then the two men looked directly at each other for the first time since their encounter in the orchard.

'You mean you *know* where the next … er … apparitions are to be found?'

Emellan nodded his head.

'I can make a fairly accurate guess. To within several kilometres.'

Their eyes locked and glittered. Emellan could hardly bring himself to say the words. He swallowed hard.

'Do you think your aunt and uncle would lend us the capital?'

'I think,' nodded Hebbel, 'that they would.'

NOTICE IN THE BLEUWBOCKEN PRESS

The small village of Kleinebocken has become the latest centre of activity for numerous spiritualists and seekers of the paranormal. In the past few months there have been over seventy reported encounters with 'the other side' and twenty-four physical manifestations which we do not hesitate to call ghosts.

Local hotel owners Gertrude and Auguste Hebbel are delighted. 'We only moved here a year ago,' they said in an exclusive interview, 'and the village was rather run down. We were expecting a quiet retirement. I think we'll have to put that off now, for at least a couple of years!'

Emellan carefully glued the clipping into his album. It was fat with such reports, as was the account that Emellan had opened at the bank. He affectionately patted his old prototype seismograph sitting on the floor beside his desk.

'Not long, old friend, not long,' he murmured, glancing at the row of shiny new seismographs he had constructed over the past few years. 'We'll show them. We'll show them yet.'

He turned back to the large map he had unfolded on the desk. A red line ran from Arnheiner to Bleuwbocken and up to the coast. He followed it with his fingers almost to the rim of the Black Sea, took a pen and marked the spot with a large *X*.

'Goodbye, ghosts,' he murmured. 'Let the Light of Science at last shine.'

He blew his nose into his handkerchief which smelled strongly of the camphor to which he had become addicted, leaned back in his chair, and laughed and laughed until the wooden legs began to creak. Borzac opened his old eyes at the unaccustomed sound, stretched like a lazy sail in a slackening wind, sneezed twice and, like the sensible creature he was, went back to sleep.

Crossing the Blue Beyond

When they come for me, I'm still sitting by the lake, the rocks scattered about my feet. I ruined every drill-bit I owned, and broke the brace in two trying to hole them through. I needed soft sea sandstone, not this dark schist that the devil has thrown across the landscape with its winks of mica casting a mirror to the moon. I can hear them crashing through the woods, probably trying to walk in twos as they've been trained to do, getting stuck on the bramble and burrs. It doesn't always pay to stick to regulations. I'm hoping the blackthorn is good and sharp enough to tear their serge. I've seen the shrike hang its songbird larder there, so it should do the job and rip and scratch as I would like to do myself. I've always hated uniforms and chucked mine down the first coal-pit I could find the second I was out the compound gate.

It's rather unfortunate I'm still here. The plan was to be at the bottom of the lake by now, but I couldn't get the string to stay wrapped around the stones. I wasted a lot of time going back home and ferreting out a load of rotten old sacking from underneath the sink. I had to avoid my mother, who was hanging out the washing, and my father, who was busy splitting logs with a sharp axe. I'd had thoughts about that axe, but couldn't figure out a foolproof way of getting a hard enough swing to guarantee severance and not just agonising and debilitating pain. I've written them each a short letter, which is rather ironic considering what got me into trouble in the first place. There's only a few words in each. It's hard to explain just exactly why I'm leaving them, so I haven't. I just said I would miss them and apologised for getting things in such a mess.

Anyhow, I got the sacking, avoided the parents and the weeping a last meeting would bring, though I thought my heart would break when I saw mother holding her hands against her back to ease the pain. I couldn't help her now or ever, except by lifting my chin and carrying out my plan. The idea was to put the sacking around the stones and use the rope for drawstrings. It took ages to disentangle the cats-cradle and get the right ropes around my ankles, and when I finally stood up and started forward, half the sacking bags ripped open or got caught on the roots coming up from the bank, and I ended up facedown in bogbean and nettles, cursing.

I realised my mistake almost immediately – I'd started too far back, leaving well over two yards to cover before I got to the water's edge. At first I was going to launch myself off the big ash that split in two last winter, half of it falling across the water like a pier. But it was harder than it looked, walking a slime-backed bole stabbed along its length with splintered branches, carrying a load of stones in your arms, sweat pouring into your eyes so you can hardly see. I got halfway out before teetering into a skid and belly-splatting into the water. By Christ but it was cold! It knocked the breath clean out of me, and before I knew what I was doing, my arms and legs were flailing like wind-bells in a hard breeze. I sat gasping on the bank, clutching my chest, feeling my blood withdrawing suddenly from my extremities then slowly surging back. I thought of Easter when we hang those bells from the trees, let them sing the joy of resurrection after we had long gone. I should have put one up before I left, an echo of my life. But of course I hadn't. We always think of these things too late, the finishing touches that would have made the situation a better statement of intent, a better full-stop to the sentence instead of the words just petering out in a strangled line. I sat there steaming in the morning sun, regretting so many things.

It goes without saying that I lost my rocks and had to start looking for them all over again. Which is when I heard the soldiers crashing their way through the woods.

I'd done my stint like everyone else – two years in the Guard for the People's Defence, followed by two years down the mines. I'd hit lucky on the latter – the salt-mines are hell. You're rubbed raw beneath your overalls, eyes red-rimmed, hands being quietly skinned by the constant ritch-ratch of salt-dust upon your skin. And then some doctor, who'd been found forging iodine prescriptions and was now doing five years, noticed that though the workers were slowly being de-gloved of skin and were sore as buggery, there was absolutely no infection whatsoever. The Authorities don't care much for lippy workers, but they're constantly grubbing around for ways to save money, and the doctor presented the perfect solution: turn the old salt-mine into a hospital. This they did, and laid out their patients on slabs of ore, chiselled the walls and tunnels to take gurneys, made doors and skylights. The main objective was achieved and the bills for disinfectant plummeted. The disgraced doctor was rewarded by removal to the Coal Mines, which if you've ever worked in a salt-mine you'll know is a big improvement, and was put on the same shift as me.

We didn't talk much – pick-axing takes up most of your time in the mines, or loading the trolleys, or hauling them up to the surface because the winch has broken again for lack of oil. We occasionally shared cigarettes and cups of cold tea in our break, but mostly we just exchanged a quiet nod. Then one night as we were trudging back up the tracks because the lift ropes had snagged, one of the surface workers let the trolley down, not realising we were on our way up. As soon as we heard the rumble and shriek of wheels on the track and saw the shadow hurtling down from above, we all flung ourselves to one side or the other. Apart from the boy whose leg was in a splint where he'd broken it last year and it hadn't been properly set. He got the strap-buckle caught in the rails and though he jumped like the rest of us, his leg stayed behind – at least until the trolley hit, when it snapped off at the knee and went rolling off on its own. The boy just sat there with his mouth wide open looking at his leg bouncing down the hill, rather neatly staying within the tracks. For a few moments no-one spoke, then there was pandemonium. Someone scrambled to the shaft-head and began furiously ringing the bell to alert the overseer to an accident, and everyone else started shouting and waving their arms around. The boy was still staring blankly after his amputated leg when someone shoved me roughly to one side, and the doctor barged through and knelt down beside the boy.

'You,' he said, looking right at me, 'go down there and fetch his leg. And you,' he prodded the closest man to him, 'give me your belt. If anyone's got handkerchiefs or a clean section of shirt, give them to me now. The rest of you go and get some prop boards so we can carry the boy up, and someone get a bucket of water.'

We stood stupidly for a second, then we all started running off or ripping up clothes. I watched for a moment as the doctor started tightening the belt about the boy's thigh, then I turned and headed into the tunnel, searching the gloom for a glint of splint or the white flash of skin.

Supper was late that night, and when we finally sat around the fire with our bowls of stew, most of us were dog-tired. By sundown nearly everyone had gone off to the bunkhouse to kip, with only a few of us staying to drink stewed tea which was black with dregs and tasted of coal. We chatted quietly, talking about the boy and his bad luck. His family had been caught smuggling chicken-feed over the border and the whole lot of them had been sent to the mines. He hadn't seen his parents since he'd got here, didn't even know to which section they'd been assigned. His two sisters had been sent to the salt and he only found out one of them had fallen down a shaft and bust her neck three months after they'd shoved her under a pile of stones and called it a grave. Then he'd gone and got his leg in the way of his pick-axe, which was hardly surprising considering the size of the thing. They really ought to provide smaller ones for the children. We all thought ourselves unlucky, but talking about that boy made us feel oddly better about our own situations, and a little guilty at the same time. Rather him than me, we all thought, and better one boy suffers than that the misery is spread around in equal parts. We felt ashamed to think such thoughts and tried to cover up by talking about what we did before, and how some of us ended up here. Some, like me, were doing our service; others had been caught thieving or smuggling or working the black market. A few, the ones with the small blue crosses tattooed on their cheeks, had been convicted of political agitation or reactionary activity against the good of the state. Mostly these ones were quiet and stuck to themselves. We'd been told we weren't to talk to them except in cases of emergency, like the boy's accident tonight, so it was unusual to find such a mix of us around the fire. We began to wonder what life would be like when we got out – where we would go, what we would do. We talked of the families we had left behind, our homes, our villages. We whispered about how things had got to change, made erratic plans to meet up and make a break for the border. When we saw the doctor coming back from the salt-mine hospital, we could see he was heading straight for the bunkhouse and I was elected to intercept and find out the news.

'How's the boy?' I asked. He looked tired and grey; the skin below his eyes had swollen between the creases.

'We lost his leg,' was all he said as he began to climb the steps. I said nothing, remembering it sticking out from underneath the trolley when it finally crashed into the buffers, how the splint had broken off, exposing a hairless calf above the boot, its lace still perfectly tied. How I'd picked it up and smartly dropped it, startled by the warmth and weight, horrified at the trickle of blood seeping from its neck. How I'd almost vomited right on top of it but managed to turn my head away just in time.

'Oh, wait,' the doctor had reached the bunkhouse door, his hand on the latch when he turned. 'I forgot. This is yours.'

He handed me the bundle he'd been carrying. It was my coat. I'd thrown it over the boy's leg and rolled it up so I could forget what was inside, a fat sausage-roll held at arm's length, dripping all the way up the shaft, dripping all the way to hospital.

'You'll probably have to clean it,' he said, and went inside. I watched him go and held the coat with the least amount of contact I could manage. Within two minutes it was burning on the fire. And that was how we met properly, the doctor and me. Two days later he brought me another coat. It was shabby and had patches on the elbows and the pockets had all been sewn up, but at least it was warm.

'I never thanked you,' he said, handing the jacket over.

'It doesn't matter,' I said, thinking: nothing much matters

125

at all.

'It mattered,' said the doctor as if he'd read my thoughts. 'Everything matters, even in here.'

Sitting here now, by the solemn blue of the lake, leaves wreathed about its edges, watching the dragonflies waiting for the sun to come and warm their wings, I wonder if he was right. I wonder if he would have been proud of me, if he would have shaken my hand and said I had done the right thing. If we would have clinked our glasses in solidarity and said 'To Freedom!'

I try and remember exactly what I wrote in that letter to the newspaper, about the boy and the trolley, but I was very drunk. So drunk I actually staggered down the street and posted it before I changed my mind. Which of course I did, and morning found me racing down to that post-box, coat flying, stubble rough, breath stale. I stood there impotent, hammering on its shiny red head, but it was too late, and the letter had long been collected and left.

I'd only been out of the mines a few months, back home to family and friends, and the girl I was supposed to marry next year, after she'd reached twenty-one and I had a position with the farming co-op. I'd always liked farming, and the thought that what I'd planted in the seedbed – the carrots and cucumbers, marrows, sunflowers, beetroot, radishes – the thought that they would all grow up and I would never see them, never smell their fresh rawness, never have the pleasure of pulling the first fruit from the tree, brought such a lump to my throat that I had to screw my fists to my eyes to stop myself wailing right there in the street by the post-box. I knew what I'd done, and that for once, it mattered. Seditious Publishing brings a statutory ten years – not that my letter was ever published. Frankly, I'm staggered anyone managed to make out any of the words. My hand hadn't been very steady at the time, and the ink had been blurred by tears. Maybe the boy's bad luck had rubbed off on me. I hadn't even put a stamp on the envelope.

I can hear the shouts of the Guards getting closer. I wonder if

I'll ever know who was right, the doctor or me, and whether everything matters, or nothing matters at all. Either way, it's all or nothing now and I'm not going back to the mines. I remember asking the doctor what would happen to the boy now he had lost a leg.

'Plenty people have lost legs,' he said. 'It doesn't make you any less than what you were. Haven't you ever lost anything?' he asked. 'Sometimes it makes you more.'

I'd laughed out loud at that, and he just smiled and rolled me a cigarette.

'Only another two hours,' I said, wondering what we'd be getting for dinner. God knows why – it was always stew and a lump of bread and a massive tureen of thick coal-dusted tea.

'Only another two years,' said the doctor, lighting his fag.

'What will you do when you get out?' I asked, breathing deep, feeling the smoke burning my throat.

'I'll never get out,' said the doctor.

And he was right. Emphysema. Dead before Christmas. I felt like I'd lost a leg when he was gone.

I thought about him a lot when I got home.

I think that was why I wrote the letter.

Why I am here now.

Why I am running up the fallen ash clutching a couple of rocks.

Why I am leaping out into the deep blue beyond, my heart battering at my chest, hoping there will be nothing on the other side of death – except perhaps the doctor, and forgiveness.

Types of Everlasting Rest

If you've ever had to cut a camel in half by its hump, you'll know not to do it again, except in extremity. The pelt is terrible tough and it stinks. Not very bloody, is all you can say good about it. But in a snow-blizzard you need fat and when a halved-hump's all you've got, you take it, even though it tastes like unboiled lard and is the kind of nasty yellow you don't even want to think about. They don't keep water in those humps: that stays in the stomach, which is handy in the desert as it comes already bagged. This isn't the desert, though deserted it might be. This is the end of the Lena River Valley, straggling its last few hundred miles of arctic tundra before seeping, exhausted, into the Laptev Sea. Almost two thousand miles back, where the Lena lapped its way out of the Baikal Mountains, camels are quite common. Surprisingly they don't seem to mind the snow. I gather their innards can cope with extremes. Unlike mine. It seems foolish now to have undertaken this trip to walk from the source of the Lena to its end. Great scenery, but far too hard and far too long. Why couldn't I just have got the boat? Where the Lena ends, I'll probably just lie down and die. I never thought I'd have to eat camel hump. I'm not sure there's going to be anywhere else to go after all this.

'I am the man named Ullendorff Bergen and I am facing a desolate road.'

These are the words my guide taught me before digging me into a snow cave and setting off for help. Apparently it amounts to 'Save Me' in the Yakut language. I mumble it over and over again, in case some reindeer-herder happens upon me, or a bear-hunter comes to knock on my snowy door:

Ullendorff Bergen dien kihibin, khardariilaakh aiannaakh.
Ullendorff Bergen dien kihibin, khardariilaakh aiannaakh.

What kind of a language is that? Oddly similar to Dutch, I think, with all those double *A*'s.

At the rear of the cave is the stony bank I've been propped

against for the last twenty-four hours, bits of bone sticking into my back. God knows what this animal is – its thigh bones arch over me like cathedral doors and we never found its head yet, despite five yards of digging. It still had some meat on it when we saw a hoof sticking out from its deep-frozen grave, and after we'd hacked a bit off with an ice-axe and roasted it on the fire, it tasted not too bad. Rather peppery and hard like cheese rind, and like cheese rind it takes a lot of chewing. Which is good – generates a little heat in your throat and makes it easier to swallow and breathe. Never knew how hard it could be to drag a bit of oxygen from the frozen air. Don't know the temperature. The mercury's been frozen solid in the thermometer since last week. Basically it averages bloody freezing and always the wrong side of zero. Leave your foot outside overnight, and in the morning it might as well be gone.

And so was Khalymar, the herdsman, and he'd taken all the camels with him.

Bastard.

Which is how we've ended up as we are: me frozen to a bank in the snow cave, peeing down my leg because I can't get up, sadly savouring the momentary warmth, and Hadak, my guide, having left and gone for help. He strapped on the skis and slid off into the morning. I would've gone with him, but my body kept veering off to one side and couldn't realistically go any further than where it already was. All those hours of practice on the ski-slopes wasted. But there it was. I could've ridden if we'd still had the camels, but the only one the bastard left was the one we'd already eaten. Walking was impossible in the wind and the snow. Sticking to a wall and having a cave built over me was the only option. I practice my lines again, but all that comes out is *Urf de kakki anorak*. It's all my frozen mouth can manage, and I don't suppose that means anything at all.

Urf rak-kak probably doesn't either, but twelve hours in and that's all I've got left.

It's dark outside; I can feel it. The sounds are different, more clean and clear. Elks coughing in the swamps. A wolf somewhere, far away; an owl close by. I hear its wings sweeping over my small snow mountain. I remember the days far back along the riverbank when the sun still shone and things were green. We saw a butterfly unfurl from a flower, wings as white as clouds. Khalymar went to squash it but Hadak held fast to his elbow.

'It might be the soul of a child,' he said whilst Khalymar wrestled back his arm.

'One less mouth to feed,' the camel-herder said and turned away.

We should have guessed his treachery then.

It's dark inside. The candle has burnt down and I can't move to light another, though Hadak left me a neat pile of tallow and a tinder-flint. The bitterns and bustards are calling through the frozen reeds. They sound like I feel, wailing in sorrow in the darkness. I hear the wolf again and everything stands still until it's gone. I wonder if it's the last thing I will ever hear.

It isn't, and the next thing I know there's a sort of tapping on the roof of my cave and a sprinkle of snow as something pokes through. *Rak-rak*, I try to say, the last of the Yakut message my mouth can manage, frozen closed within my beard, and no sound anyway appears to escape my throat. A pinpoint of light pinions my foot and I hear a voice. I try to croak again but I've all frozen up, inside and out, even my eyelids are stuck at half-mast as though I've already died. Much more noise and much more light; blocks of snow being hacked away and removed. Someone drags me over to a fire. Someone takes off my sodden jacket and wraps me in their own. I feel the heat begin to melt my skin. My boots are taken off, then my trousers, and someone washes the stink and stain from me, rubs the blood back into my legs, covers me with a slaughterhouse of furs to replace the cold night of my cave. I sleep and sleep and when I awake, it's dark again and I can hear the wolf back on its hill. There's a tin of tea still warming on the fire, and some meat blackening in the embers. I'm too tired to move, but there's something familiar about that wheezing snore, about that smell. I crane my neck a little under my mountain of dead animals and open an eye. My companion is clad in a camel-skin coat, and there's only one man around here would wear that.

The bastard came back.

In the morning he cleans my hands and feet then re-swaddles them in fur; he lifts tea to my lips, he chops the meat into bits with his sharp knife and feeds me them from the tip. He ties the biggest furs around my body and slings me between the humps of a camel, my arms and legs hanging like braces of pheasant down the camel's flanks. He tells me it will keep the blood pooled in my extremities and stop the frostbite getting any worse. Then we plod, plod, plod, on and on and Khalymar talks to me so I've things to think about and keep my brain from turning to stone. I find out that Khalymar never left us at all. I find out that he told Hadak he was taking the camels through the valley where they would be more comfortable for the night and find grazing for a day or two, where the snow was thinner and blown back from the grass by the wind; that he would be back as soon as the weather let up. I find out that Hadak took the skis and all my bags and money. I find out that it was Hadak, the man who saves butterflies, who had left me to die.

My God, but you don't know how much you itch until you haven't got nails to scratch with! Three days ago we reached a village and Khalymar sold his camels and bought a boat and threw me in it, still bounden in my furs. I'd seen the doctor when we'd reached the village, and by then I had thawed enough to tell him my tale. We spoke in broken Russian in single-syllable words and got the gist across: Baikal, Lena, Journey, Book, Travel, Long, Snow, Cold, Rescue. Sad that my adventure could be summed up by so little. Sadder still that when the Doctor gently peeled away my gloves to assess the damage, the most part of my fingers stayed behind, and likewise my feet. There was nothing to be done except board the boat and carry on, reach a bigger town which had a proper hospital and hopefully a train to take me home. A huge crowd gathered as I was carried down to the black-boled pier, the whole village turned out, waving bottles of vodka at us and singing songs. The Doctor gave me his address so I could send some more up-to-date textbooks. The ones he had were so ancient they recommended a mixture of antimony and arsenic as a cure for frostbite, and neither one of us could see the sense in that.

It was still cold, lying in the basin of that boat. There's a kind of cold you get when you can't remember what it's like to be warm, and doubt you'll ever get the chance again. The Doctor recommended as much movement as possible, so I tried to paddle my arms and legs, but was hampered by the weight of the furs. The nights and days passed as a log floats down a stream – smoothly, but with no fixed direction. I had the feeling we spun in the current now and then and frequently felt we were travelling the wrong way round. My head did not seem to be functioning all that well and often I just drifted away, staring at the clouds or the stars or the canvas tent above my body.

It was a strange boat; I had the wits to notice that. It was made of logs, roughly planed and doweled together with thick pins, their width still visible between the boards. The sail was small, made of stretched skin, and the boat went with the sluggish current, directed by a small set of oars attached to the back of the boat. Bundles of reeds lined the blank boards. There were no seats nor storage places, only that tent of canvas strained taut over the middle, hiding my body from the worst of the wind and sleet. I heard Khalymar laughing with the boatmen who strung fishing lines out behind them and hauled up sterlet and roach which they cooked in the oil-can brazier nailed to the bow. When they'd eaten enough, they pushed the fish inside a reed-bundle and used it to damp down the fire, leaving the fish inside to smoke. The smell was of earth and warm moss and the slow sweetness of curing flesh. Or so I imagined. It's hard to smell anything when your nose has got jammed between the bottom boards of a boat and is anyway nowhere near your face.

It was back at the village when I was being carried to the pier that the tip of my nose fell off. Just like that – a treacherous black marble rolling in the snow. Someone picked it up and threw it on board behind me as if it were a charm for good luck. I gazed back at the doctor and he just shrugged. I supposed there was nothing else he could do. The crew tried to help, but those Laptev boys knew no other treatment than to smear cow-lard across my face and cover it with a fox-tail to keep out the worsening cold. They were used to it I supposed, and they didn't even put their gloves on till we'd crossed another line of latitude when the ice began to wrinkle out from underneath the banks and the surface of the Lena gradually slowed and closed around us. The boat still moved, but barely, and the men took up the oars to power us through. The ice wept as we broke it apart and sighed closed behind us after we had gone. For more than half the year the Lena waters slow down to freezing and stop altogether, so I guessed we were lucky we got there when we did. Overhead, huge clouds of cranes and swans swept low over the landscape, the breeze of their wings blowing over our faces, making the lace of ice across the river shift and sing. Curlews called and rose in nervous alarm as we passed them by on the river banks, and the farther we went, the wider became the river, spreading itself thin over marsh and bog-meadow, the ice thickening inch by inch, mile by mile. The river split and spilled around a multitude of islands, some huge, some tiny islets of trees, some overlooked as fallen boulders in the two hundred mile sprawl of the watery bay. The crew and Khalymar slew the boat always to the west and we rounded the river to Bulkur, which was our journey's end. Two thousand four hundred miles I had travelled, and it had cost me dear.

I saw Khalymar right and bought him a brand new boat, and in summer off he went upriver to home and a new life giving fishing trips to tourists and showing them the seals on the shores of the Baikal. As for me, I never got home. What was left of me stayed on by the Laptev Sea. I didn't want to leave the atrocious cold of winter days and the bright white light of summer nights. The tundra tolls behind me and around me for a hundred thousand miles and is all kinds of Everlasting

133

Types of Everlasting Rest

Rest. That's what they call it here, because its seasons never change and always follow each other like an elk eating its tail. You might try to change it but you never will, though it might well change you. And so it seems. I don't know whatever else I left on the Lena, besides my fingers and toes and the end of my nose. What I do know is that I can never leave it for long. I'm too tired to retrace my steps and try to go back. I've aged too much to do all that again. I've gained my goal, and now I've realised what Khalymar most likely knew all along: that when it comes down to it, you are what you are and you're just like everyone else.

So I sit here by my fire, skins of sea-otters wrapped around my knees and shoulders, my book open but unread on the table, thinking of all I have gained and all I have lost.

In the end, we're all the same.

Just another mouth to feed.

And there's a kind of peace in that. I go to turn a page but the prosthesis slips upon the paper and the book falls to the floor. I don't mind. I let it lie. I blow out the lamp and gaze through the open window at all the stars singing silently with their black lips, see the Lena spool her way across the plains, feel her ice around my neck and beg her, beg her to take me with her across the thousand miles of tundra I know I will never see.

I remember when Khalymar told me about that butterfly. It was a moth, he said; a ghost-moth is what he called it. They drink the tears of your animals at night. They pass on infections. They kill cattle by sucking at their open wounds.

We should have let him kill it after all.

Give it some of that everlasting rest.

Fiction from Two Ravens Press

Love Letters from my Death-bed
Cynthia Rogerson

There's something very strange going on in Fairfax, California. Joe Johnson is on the hunt for dying people while his wife stares into space and flies land on her nose; the Snelling kids fester in a hippie backwater and pretend that they haven't just killed their grandfather; and Morag, multi-bigamist from the Scottish Highlands, makes some rash decisions when diagnosed with terminal cancer by Manuel – who may or may not be a doctor. Meanwhile, the ghost of Consuela threads her way through all the stories, oblivious to the ever-watching Connie – who sees everything from the attic of the Gentle Valleys Hospice.

Cynthia Rogerson's second novel is a funny and life-affirming tale about the courage to love in the face of death.

'Witty, wise and on occasions laugh-aloud funny. A tonic for all those concerned with living more fully while we can.' **Andrew Greig**
'Her writing has a lovely spirit to it, an appealing mixture of the spiky and the warm.' **Michel Faber**

£8.99. ISBN 978-1-906120-00-9. Published April 2007.

Nightingale
Peter Dorward

On the second of August 1980, at 1pm, a bomb placed under a chair in the second class waiting room of the international railway station in Bologna exploded, resulting in the deaths of eighty-five people. Despite indictments and arrests, no convictions were ever secured. Exactly a year before the bombing, a young British couple disembarked at the station and walked into town. He – pale-blue eyes, white collarless shirt, baggy green army surplus trousers – and twenty yards behind him, the woman whom, in a couple of years he will marry, then eventually abandon. He is Don, she is Julia. Within twenty-four hours she'll leave for home, and he will wander into a bar called the *Nightingale* – and a labyrinthine world of extreme politics and terrorism. More than twenty years later their daughter Rosie, as naïve as her father was before her, will return to the city, and both Don – and his past – will follow...

'Nightingale is a gripping and intelligent novel; it takes an unsentimental and vivid look at the lives of a small group of Italian terrorists and the naïve Scottish musician who finds himself in their midst in Bologna in

1980. Full of authentic detail and texture, Nightingale *is written with clarity and precision. Peter Dorward tells this tragic story with huge confidence and verve.'* **Kate Pullinger**

£9.99. ISBN 978-1-906120-09-2. Published September 2007.

Parties
Tom Lappin

Gordon yearns for a little power; Richard wishes reality could match the romantic ideal of a perfect pop song; Grainne wants life to be a little more like Tolstoy. Beatrice looks on and tries to chronicle the disappointment of a generation measuring the years to the end of the century in parties.

Parties is a black comedy about young people getting older, and learning to be careful what they wish for, lest they end up finding it.

£9.99. ISBN 978-1-906120-11-5. Published October 2007.

Prince Rupert's Teardrop
Lisa Glass

The story of a damaged woman's relationship with her mother, a nonagenarian Armenian haunted by the genocide of her people by the Turkish Army early in the twentieth century. When her mother disappears, it is left to this most unreliable and unpredictable of daughters to try to find her, in this moving, lyrical, and provocative work.

'Lisa Glass writes with dazzling linguistic exuberance and a fearless imagination.' **R.N. Morris**

£9.99. ISBN 978-1-906120-15-3. Published November 2007.

The Most Glorified Strip of Bunting
John McGill

The US North Polar expedition of 1871-73 was a disaster-strewn adventure that counts amongst the most bizarre and exciting in the annals of Arctic exploration. *The Most Glorified Strip of Bunting* is a fictionalised account of its events, based on the firsthand accounts of the participants. A recurring theme of the novel is the clash of two civilisations – Inuit and European – and the mutual misunderstanding and hostility that arise from it.

£9.99. ISBN 978-1-906120-12-2. Published November 2007.

Short Fiction

Highland Views: a collection of stories by David Ross.
£7.99. ISBN 978-1-906120-05-4. Published April 2007.

Military jets exercise over Loch Eye as a seer struggles to remember his vision; the honeymoon is over for workers down at the Nigg yard, and an English incomer leads the fight for independence both for Scotland and for herself... This debut collection of stories provides an original perspective on the Highlands, subtly addressing the unique combination of old and new influences that operate today.

'I'm a big fan. A fine organic collection that advances a viewpoint, culture and history quite other than the urban central belt that still lopsidedly dominates recent Scottish literature.' **Andrew Greig**
'A view of the Highlands with a strong element of political and social comment. Ross explores these concerns in convincingly human terms through the lives of his characters.' **Brian McCabe**

Riptide: an anthology of new prose and poetry from the Highlands and Islands. Edited by Sharon Blackie & David Knowles.

This diverse collection of new fiction and poetry from the Highlands & Islands showcases the work of established writers and new names to watch.

'...a force of creation, the kind of irresistible tide into which we should dip.' **The Scotsman**

£8.99. ISBN 978-1-906120-02-3. Published April 2007.

Poetry

Castings: by Mandy Haggith.
£8.99. ISBN 978-1-906120-01-6. Published April 2007.
Leaving the Nest: by Dorothy Baird.
£8.99. ISBN 978-1-906120-06-1. Published July 2007.
The Zig Zag Woman: by Maggie Sawkins.
£8.99. ISBN 978-1-906120-08-5. Published September 2007.
In a Room Darkened: by Kevin Williamson.
£8.99. ISBN 978-1-906120-07-8. Published October 2007.

For more information on these and other titles, and for extracts and author interviews, see our website.

**Titles are available direct from the publisher at
www.tworavenspress.com
or from any good bookshop.**